PRAISE FOR PILLEATER

"perhaps I'm a 'normie' then, because it is certainly not good enough for me." - Adam Parfrey

"lolol asian pill. idk man shit is crazy in general right now. wild times." - Sam Hyde

"The alt-right is atrocious and the fact that you're giving those morons oxygen is more than enough to dissuade me from appearing on your show." - Chris Korda

"Pilleater embodies the harmonic whimsicality that Elliot Rodger might have realized, had he channeled his emotions more constructively and stuck to Asian chicks."
- Brandon Adamson, author of *Beatnik Fascism*

"Pilleater inherently understands the alt-right and alt-left are empty signifiers of the same collective – rudderless, underdeveloped males. *Almond Eyes, Baby Face* dares to envision a newly-grafted race, one willing to pick up arms for its survival. It is refreshing to see such dangerous thoughtcrime still being practiced in these ultra-puritanical times." - James Nulick, author of *Valencia*

"Pilleater, a true literary outsider, explores themes and ideas that are totally outside of what we're accustomed to expect from literary fiction. He is an absolute original and a unique voice in contemporary literature. Shake off your boring vanilla expectations and experience the world of Trip—if you dare!" - Casper, editor of fluland.com

"The leading Asian-Aryan Alt-Right intellectual of his generation." - Luke Ford

"Well, I like that is good, clean writing, no literary pretension. Your own original manifesto on Asian girls, a subject I know little about. It would be too much work for me to critique, something I never like to do. For all I know, you could have a hit on your hands." - Josh Alan Friedman, author of *Black Cracker*

"Pilleater is one of the more vital and interesting voice of the alt right and new counter culture. He has cross platform talents from pod casting to video blogging and his new book form literary endeavors are well worth your time to take a look at." - Richard Wolstencroft

"Where I can support Asian-Aryanism fully and unequivocally, however, is in viewing Asians and white as having largely emerged under the same hyper-social evolutionary pressures, and to therefore see the problems facing whites as problems which already - and even more so in the future - are felt by Asians." - HAarlem VEnison

trip

by pilleater

Choam Charity Publishing #002
Philadelphia, PA USA

ISBN-10: 0-9989203-1-2
ISBN-13: 978-0-9989203-1-3

Second Edition,
Second Printing, 2017

Printed in the USA.

Front cartoon design by Piemboons.
http://piemboons.tumblr.com

For

Z.

TRIP

As the colors swim in circles
And rhythms shimmer through the chandeliers
As the gods send gifts of balance
And things of distance become things of near
As the sky reaches burnout
And the crowds disappear
In the temple I'll be waiting
For my angel to appear

-Cause & Effect

1.

"God, you're such a bad driver."

"Why do you say that?"

"The left lane is where you speed up. You don't fucking go 55 on the left."

"What the hell am I supposed to do?"

"Fucking speed up!"

Tom was pumping the car with gas at a station out in the middle of Arizona. Daisy looked upset.

She said, "Well, I don't know. Do you want me to be the driver, or do you want your sorry ass on the wheel again?"

"Gee, I am not so sure. Sometimes, I am afraid that if we have kids, our children are going to have the bad driver gene, thanks to you."

Tom looked down on the ground like he was actually sad.

"What's that supposed to mean?" Daisy said in a confused manner.

"You know, race mixing is bad. I think all my white nationalist friends are right. Half white-Asian offspring have identity issues, are mentally unstable, and don't have someone to look up to."

He stopped pumping once the LCD screen reached $19.65.

"Shut up," she said back at Tom. "You're with me because you don't want to put real effort into a normal white girl. That's what all white guys do. Get all emo and make up stuff!"

"Now you're going all tiger-mom on me!"

"Are you going to drive, or not?"

"I am you fucking dumb chink!" he said with a smirk on his face.

Daisy gasped with her mouth wide open. "Fuck you, you fucking cracker!" she said with a chuckle.

They were playing like they always do. Both had got used to talking to each other like abusive jocks on a football team. They never meant what they said... or did they?

6:42PM. The sun was slowly setting. The sky turning from its orange to a deep purple.

Tom had to go inside the 7-Eleven for some cash. Daisy waited for him in the car. She lit her cigarette in the car. Usually she doesn't smoke. But for an adventure like this, who knows what's going to happen.

Tom strutted in the store like a bad cartoon character. Like a doo-wop, googie kind of bully, sort of like Fonzie. He spotted the ATM machine.

Really bad music played over the telecom.

...*Information Society - Pure Energy.*

"What a great song. I remember that song from a few years ago... on YouTube. Yeah, that guy Kurt, he did some songs for that video game Gex, right? So strange. I love his different colored hair and... that video. I wonder if Mindless Self-Indulgence were into Information Society? They have the same aesthetics going on."

...That thought was racing through Tom's head.

Tom pressed the buttons on the touch screen. The machine asked for his MasterCard. Tom slid in the card, and quickly took it back out. It didn't work. He tried again. Didn't work again.

...Oh yeah. It was one of those new cards with the chip in it. He had to shove the card in the machine, and then wait for about five seconds (and counting) before the machine read it. Sliding the card inside the machine again, he waited. It was reading it. ...Good.

This is from... Primary checking? Saving? Checking, yes. Deposit, Withdraw? Withdraw. Withdrawing the amount of $10-1000?

"Where is the $40 button?" he thought to himself. His finger hovered around like a bee about to sting a person. $40. Confirmed.

PLEASE WAIT, the machine insisted.

3

Tom waited. And waited. Wait, now the machine displayed, PLEASE REMOVE CARD BEFORE CASH IS DISPENSED.

Yeah, the new chip thingy. "I hope I don't pull it out and then the security service at MasterCard tells me my card is frozen. I am not a thief. Just stupid at working with this thing."

Tom took the card. The machine ticked a bit, and two twenty dollar bills fell out of the machine. He thought about something before he grabbed the money.

"Wait a second. How much do I have? If I took out forty, and I have about... $80 left..."

Tom grabbed the money. ...Who cares? He will get an income from his trust fund in a few days. He's got money in the bank.

He counted his cash, and tucked it back into his wallet. The lyrics sang,

"I want to know! What you're thinking! There is something on your mind!"

...What a good song.

Often as was his habit, Tom pressed the red cancel button on the ATM machine a couple of times, just so no one got his card information if it's displayed on the screen. He never did get the receipts. Last time he collected his receipts, he would shove them in the pocket of his car.

Eventually, he would saved up two-years' worth of gas and ATM receipts until there was a paper nest too large for his glovebox. He never did show the receipts to his trust fund agent either. Tom made a vow a few months ago not to collect receipts anymore. Everything is electronic by the way. It doesn't matter how much money is spent. A computer can be an accountant for you.

Tom had the temptation to buy a bag of beef jerky. Something his dad would never allow him to buy if he was with him. The price was $6.78. Why not? He needed to break a single $20 bill. Tom grabbed the beef jerky and threw it down at the cash register.

A Hispanic man was alone in the store. "Hey pops, is that it?"

"Yes sir," Tom said, passing his twenty-dollar bill. $20? Yes. The cash register opened, the man quickly popped back with different bills. The twenty-dollar bill went under the register. Quickly, Tom was done in under a minute. A quarter spit out the change dispenser. He was handed a few dollar bills and a ten dollar one.

"Thank you, sir," Tom said back.

"Have a good day," the sleepy Hispanic man said.

Tom finally got out of the store. Some bogus acoustic song started to play after Information Society.

The sky was still orange. The car was still there. Daisy was done smoking. She was staring at her phone, like most loner people do to feel that their time is being occupied.

Tom hopped in the driver's seat. "Wait, am I supposed to drive?"

Daisy looked back at him dumbfounded.

"I thought I was supposed to drive?"

"No, no. I'm driving!"

Daisy saw the bag of beef jerky Tom brought from the 711. She examined the bag and was about to open it.

"Can I have this now?"

"Sure you can!"

While she tore it, she thought of something. "Wait! ...wait-wait-wait-wait! I need something!"

"You need what?"

"I need a Monster! Do they have some?"

"Yeah, they do." Tom looked back at her.

"I can't drive unless I get a Monster."

"Wait, hold on, I am the one supposed to be driving!

"No, no. That's ok. I need a Monster and everything is okay. How much have you got?"

"Thirty something?"

Daisy reached for her pocket to grab some spare change. She reached out and gave some to Tom.

"Go back in the store and go buy me one. It's okay to spend this money!"

Tom looked at her with concern.

"Are you sure you need one? I don't get it, we're almost there." She thought about it.

"Umm... Yeah, I do need it. Get me one."

Tom didn't feel like going back in the store, but he was going to anyway.

"What do you want?"

"Green flavored," she said.

Tom got out of the car and headed into the store again to get the drink.

Daisy had two cigarettes left. She just smoked one. Looking at her lighter and cigs, she didn't think she was going to use them for any purpose but for anxiety and boredom. That last smoke was just out of habit. She had a butt cramp too.

Daisy opened the car door, and got out to stretch a bit. She turned off her phone. The sky was a deep orange. A classic scene, out in the desert. A modernized and somewhat civilized desert. Not the lone desert that if your car breaks down, you're fucked. A kind of desert with at least a phone booth every mile and gas station here and there. A unique Americana and Western kind of bumfuck.

Daisy saw the trash can. She was holding her Kools. She looked at them. Started slowly thinking about her habit. Took a deep breath. She made up her mind, and threw the cigs into the trash can. The second cig missed and fell on the ground.

The dumb gas station commercial started to play in the background. The goofy music that comes with it too. The race car bleeping noises that follow with it. *Eeep-Beep-Bleep*. Daisy looked at the TV.

"You're watching 7-Eleven TV! Proud sponsor of NASCAR!" ...and who cares? Embarrassing and abrasive to begin with.

It was getting somewhat cold. The evening was coming. The only car parked at the gas station was their own. It felt like they were in the wild.

She saw Tom finally get out of the store and come racing back to see her. The green can was in his hand. "Here you go," he said, passing the baton-like drink to her.

She looked at the drink, and then she looked back at him. He was standing above her looking at her face. She had to tell Tom something important.

She passed him back the Monster.

"I quit."

"Quit?"

"Yeah, I quit."

"Quit what?"

"I don't need caffeine or tobacco. Nope."

She looked at him with a smile.

"What do you mean? Do you want this?"

She chuckled, "you're going to have it, I thought you were driving."

Tom laughed, "Wait, what? Now you want me to drive? Ok, ok, I thought that's what we agreed on."

"I wanted you to have the drink, you're going to need it."

Both headed towards the car. Tom opened the door to the front seat.

"You know, you're totally unpredictable at times, right?

She smiled. "I care for you too. It was worth it to get it."

"I don't want to drink it now, because I feel like I will have to pee like a race horse midway."

"We are only, what, 40 minutes away?"

Tom thought about it. "Yeah, I guess you're right. I need a shot."

Tom cracked open the Monster. Daisy reached for a piece of beef jerky. The radio had on some Negrophile station. Really old and bad sounding R&B and New Jack Swing. Both had to eat before he had to focus on the road.

Tom reached for a piece of jerky to chew on. He looked at Daisy.

"The guy in the store, is this real lazy Mexican motherfucker. with a lazy eye and everything. I think he was autistic."

Daisy laughed.

Tom was curious. He had to ask her, "what's your thoughts on Mexicans?"

"What?"

"Mexicans, what do you think about them."

Daisy thought about it.

"Umm. I think they are good people. They are fine with me. They just work all the time, and I think they are second rate to blacks, you know? Black people are the worst and commit the most crimes. But I think Mexicans commit crimes when they are with Blacks."

Then Tom had to burst out,

"Yeah! Fuck niggers! Anything but being black!" he was laughing aloud. She was laughing too.

"Like, Mexicans are fine. They just try too hard to be black!" she said.

"You're right."

Tom put the keys in the car and switched into drive. He was ready to go. After another sip from the Monster, he put his foot on the pedal. Turning the wheel, he left the 7-Eleven. He rolled down the windows. There was a nice breeze in the evening. When Tom turned left or right, he always put on his blinkers, even though no one was behind him. Once on the road he drove straight forward, one direction into the abyss.

It was so nice outside. Daisy had to take some pictures for the moment. She opened her camera app, lifted her phone outside the window, and took some shots of the sky. The photos always came out grainy on her phone. Tom couldn't look at her. He was too busy focusing on the road.

The 7-Eleven was now some distance away.

Going straight, with negro music on really low. Daisy eating jerky and enjoying looking out the window like a little kid.

She said to Tom. "I am making a new vow. I am not smoking anymore. I don't need that stuff."

Tom had to look straight, but talk to Daisy as well. "That's good! Good for you!"

She said, looking down at her own self, without any eye contact. "Yeah like, I don't need any cigarettes, that stuff makes me look ugly and fat. I don't need to be a drug addict. I need to eat healthy and lose weight."

Tom gave her some advice, "Well, as long as you watch what you eat every day. The key is to lose weight by not eating that much. Don't eat like you have to and eat a lot of fruit. Also avoid sugar."

Daisy nodded her head to his advice.

"Like, I don't need to smoke because it's not worth it. I don't need it. It's too much money."

"Yeah, don't do it. I don't smoke. When you get older, you start to realize the world is limited. Better to do good things now than risk it."

"Yeah," she said back.

Daisy had another thought.

"But I will still drink. It's not like I am straight edged or anything."

Tom laughed.

"Ok. But only drink on special occasions. That's my policy. I drink when you're around."

"Yeah, like I need a drink sometimes but not all the time."

The GPS was hooked into the car. A loud robotic voice tuned in, "In-the-next-five-miles, turn right-onto-Dekalb-Exit."

"I think we are almost there," Tom said.

"This is going to be exciting," she said back. "I hope you don't fuck up this time!"

"Oh, I think I know what I am going to do!"

"Are you going to rehearse the small titty joke?"

Tom laughing again, "Yes I will!"

"You're going to go all out on it. I hope Sarah never finds out about your antics."

"Ahh, well, it's only a joke. I'm going to be all like… actual stuff people find funny on this. Less about the surrealist kind."

"Yeah, you don't want to confuse the audience."

"A bunch a normies we have tonight!"

Daisy thought about something.

"Wait, is this new material you're doing tonight? Not recycled from last time?"

"Yep! New material! I wrote a 1000-word script about it. But I generally know what I am going to talk about. Totally improvised."

"Awesome, you wrote it last night?"

"I was finishing it last night. I only wrote a few sentences. It's going to be the girls I see with guys."

Daisy burst out laughing.

"Hahah! oh shit! This is going to be major!"

As they both talked, the sky turned magenta. Almost 7 o'clock, night was fast approaching. They were almost there at the venue.

Tom turned off to the DeKalb exit.

The windows were down, the air breezing in the car. Tonight was an exciting night. It was a good night to be alive.

2.

"Turn off this Nig music!" Daisy said. Something about old black men and their voodoo chanting was ruining the mood.

The sky was a purple-blue. To be reminded of an old black guy singing at this time is like playing that same exact song the first time you have sex.

"Ok, hold on," said Tom as he fiddled with the tune dial. He directly turned the dial to 103.3. Since they were in a different state, it was no longer the college radio station they usually listened to. Rather, it was bland country, pop music.

"What CDs do we have?" he asked.

Daisy had something in mind.

"We've already listened to Depeche Mode too much. But… I don't think we listened to this one…"

Daisy had a blank CD-R. She inserted the disc into the car's player.

The radio went silent for a bit. The CD was loading.

"What did you put in?" he asked.

The electro drums came blaring on.

It was that song.

Do I look like a slut? Ah-uh. Shut up.

"This song is so funny!" Daisy laughed.

The very memorable synth line. The funny lyrics about sex. Avenue D was avant-garde for its time.

"This song is so old. It feels like yesterday I was in middle school."

Do I look like a slut? Is it the way I move my butt? Is it the way my jeans are cut? I don't give a fuck.

"I think the girls are so awesome and sassy," she said.

Tom was looking out the window. He had to say something funny too.

"You know, what if I told you, that Harriet Sugarcookie originally sang on this track?"

Daisy looked back, "Wait, what?"

"Yeah, Harriet Sugarcookie is singing."

"No, it's not."

"Yes, it is. Really. She does porn too and she loves to sing."

Daisy was surprised. "Really? If that is really Harriet then, oh my god, then really she is singing as an Asian porn actress!"

"Yeah, I know right?"

"I mean, if this really is her, then she would be representing all Asian hookers," she was laughing.

Tom couldn't keep it a secret.

"No, I'm kidding, that's not Harriet." He smirked.

15

Daisy turned red, though she was still smiling.

"Haha, you fucking liar. I know you were making shit up!" She punched him on the shoulder.

Tom smiled back.

A green car suddenly passed them in the opposite direction.

"Punch buggy green!" she scream in the car, and punched Tom in the head.

Tom was used to hard punches like that. Both were laughing now.

He could never beat her in the game called "Punch Buggy." She started this when they first met. Every time a car of a certain color appeared, she had to punch him and name the color of the car. Tom could only punch Daisy back if he saw the car of the same color.

. . . Or something like that. Sometimes he could punch her for the sake of a car of any color.

The GPS announced, "Turn-right-on-Fiddler-Street" and then, "your-destination-is-on-the-right."

They were almost there.

Tom replied, "I got it. I know what I am doing."

"I think you should talk about sex. Sex always makes people laugh."

"I will," Tom said.

They found their destination. *Rodman Hall*, a little venue out in the middle of nowhere with some saloon buildings here and there, It felt like they were in an industrialized, post-modern cowboy town.

Tom parked the car. "I think we should go in the back and find the guy," he said.

Tom and Daisy headed towards the back of the building to find the VIP door. A guy was sitting out front.

Tom yelled, "Yo, sir! Do you know of Steve Chowder?"

"What's that?" the sleepy man asked.

"Steve Chowder."

The sleepy man got up from the railing he sat on, and said, "Hold on one second."

The man put his head through the back doorway, and yelled, "Steve! There is a guy waiting outside for you!"

Tom and Daisy waited for a few boring seconds.

A plump man with a greasy Elvis haircut came out. He had a fat, double chin and dark facial features.

He pointed at Tom. "Tom?"

"Yeah."

"Come on in! We been waiting for you!"

That was their sign to go in. The outside world was finally dark. They entered inside a strange place.

The back room was full of clutter. Used guitars and broken drum sets sat in a desolate corner. Tom and Daisy shook hands with the nice strangers. It felt like Tom had to shake hands with every person he met inside. This gig was only for tonight. He wondered if Jake was here tonight.

They entered the green room. —A room with a couch and orange sofa no one wanted.

"Make yourself at home dude. We will be calling you, in say, 30 minutes? We got some strange weirdos in tonight that will really love what you do!"

"Alright, peace man," Tom said as the Elvis-looking manager left the room.

There was a frizzle-haired man with some strange ankh earrings and dark makeup. Obviously some goth-revival kid. Again, for the billionth time, Tom and Daisy shook their hands and made their introduction. His name was Snake.

"That's really cool, writing a book about Asian girls, dude," he said, while looking back at Daisy. She had to say something.

"I know, it's cool, right?" she asked.

"Well, how the hell do you deal with it? Is it sexist? Or..."

"No, it's not like that at all. I like how Tom expresses himself. He's not racist at all or anything like that. He loves Asian culture and I think it's true there are a lot of Americans that never acknowledge they have, —you know, —Asian girlfriends!" She laughed. Daisy was trying to make the situation more normal. Tom's avant-garde book about Asian girls was a little controversial, even for the average reader. It's why he's now hanging out with different kinds of people who understand him.

"I only looked at the book for a bit. But seriously, that one part, about you fucking a girl in the car. That's so lewd."

Tom felt embarrassed. He knows Daisy did read over his book before. That everything in the book is fictional and not really about himself.

"What, it's me really trying to express myself. I don't think Dennis Cooper or even Peter Sotos means what they write either, do they?"

Snake had a knowledge of esoteric and underground writers. "Ah shit dude, yeah, you're right. It's just written words."

Tom was able to stir down the conversation into something normal. Snake had to do something else. Oddly enough, Tom had somewhat of a celebrity background, even though most of his work was written and published online. Recently, he has been meeting people "irl" and creating a network.

Eventually Snake was gone. Tom could now sit down on the sofa and talk to Daisy. He loved Daisy so much.

He whispered into her ear. "So, how about all these weirdos tonight? That guy is so ugly!"

Daisy agreed with him by laughing.

"It felt like we entered a room full of zombies! Are we getting a hotel room after this?"

"Yeah, there's no after parties or anything. Super queer motorcycle dudes. They all probably have gay sex with each other when no one's looking."

Tom and Daisy were acting like little school children.

"At least there must be some guy with sense here."

Daisy poured herself some orange soda.

"It took so long today. I'm glad we finally made it," she said.

"Yeah, that was, like, six hours on the road today?"

"You're okay to go up tonight?"

"Yeah, sure! I will be fine! It's going to be like, what? 10 to 15 minutes?"

Tom and Daisy were both anxious from their adventure today.

A man with a long Santa Claus beard came over to get a can of orange soda too. He had on a big shirt that said "Cosmic Wimpout."

One of Tom's passions was board games. Since he was 15, he was a local game player who gamed regularly to play *Android: Netrunner* and his favorite board game, *Cosmic Encounter.* The name, "Cosmic Wimpout," was all too familiar. He had to ask the old dude about the game.

"Cosmic Wimpout! Hey man! I'm a huge fan of the game!"

The old man looked back at him. "Ha, really? I met the guys who made the game! It's such a far-out game!"

Tom and the old man were now talking like nerds on a thing no one cares about.

"Yeah, I got everything! I got the Berkeley board, the dying sun . . . . I use the Ice Pyramids to track progress on the board and make up my own rules with them," Tom boasted.

"Andrew Looney? Oh yes, what a wonderful man. I met him once before. A nice man he is. I love his pyramid games. Very nostalgic for me."

This nerd conversation didn't go anywhere. The old man had to do something else at the moment. He was working at his own job.

When the man left, Daisy had to but in, "Oh my god, that man knew everything you were talking about. Are we like, in a place full of zombie gay guys that play board games all day?"

Tom laughed. "And they do drugs, listen to The Grateful Dead and are part of the esoteric culture of Cosmic Wimpout? It's a movement!"

Both laughed together.

Tom's voice was getting hoarse from all the talking.

"My voice is getting hoarse. I hope I can do this."

"What are you going to talk about?"

"I'm going to yell like Tom Green does, and be like, that girl goes out with that girl and her titties are small!"

Daisy thought about it for a second.

"Start calmly. Be like, I was going down to this party in Philadelphia. And you know, comment how disgusting and pathetic Philadelphia is. Arizonian people don't know about that place."

"You're right."

"And then be like, so there are tons of guys in Philly with Asian girlfriends and they keep it a secret. And explain that there is this whole culture behind it all."

"Exactly."

"That's when you will all be like, this girl is a bitch. That girl is too submissive and those guys are skinheads. Those guys are pussynerds, and finally talk about how they all act together in a bar and what happens."

"Yes!"

"Like they get into a fight or some shit!"

"Yes! I like where this is going!"

Tom thought about something for a bit.

"I came up with this skit watching *Star Vs. The Forces of Evil*. That cute show on Disney, right?"

"The show you were telling me about how West Coast and Asian-Aryan it is?"

"Hell yeah. And everyone in that show, if you look at the minor characters, are either Asian or dating white guys. It's like a West Coast wet dream."

"You were telling me about this before."

"Yeah. And it's like a kids show too. But it's telling all these young kids how cool White-Asian couples act like at Stuff-White-People-Like parties. Really cool stuff like that."

"I see."

"Yeah and like, everybody wishes they could live a life like that. Including myself!"

Daisy laughed.

"We never been to California."

"We should go this week! We are so close by!"

"We should!"

The conversation digressed from comedy to real life drama. They were very close to California.

A man opened the door, looking at them with his head out.

"Alright, Tom, you ready?"

Tom shook his head up.

"Yep, I'm ready to go!"

Tom stood up.

"I'm totally ready now, Daisy."

"Did you go to the bathroom?"

Tom thought about it.

"Shit, let me go do that. Go out there and watch me!"

Tom had to kiss Daisy on the cheek.

He headed for the bathroom while Daisy went out of the room.

Tom entered the disgusting bathroom. A typical bathroom with tar on the ceiling and gross sinks. There were two stalls. Tom went into the last to take a piss. There was a classic glory hole and graffiti written all over the walls. At least three phone numbers were on the wall, all of which had the subtitle of "good head." Tom didn't bother to flush. He headed for the sink. Hardly any soap was left to wash his hands. He was excited. Only three minutes left and he was going to perform. His ADHD was ticking in. He didn't know whether to make noises like a little Gremlin or sing the Goof Troop theme song. He had to make himself feel good.

He looked at himself in the mirror.

Brown hair, brown eyes, a mustache, and goatee. He had to shave the extra hairs coming in on his neck. He swiped his hair back. He didn't put gel in his hair. If he did, he always went with a fake-Mohawk style. He didn't know much about hair design. He had his glasses on. It was best though to take them off when he performed. That way, he couldn't look people directly in the eye and pretend as if he was looking at everyone. He took off his glasses, swished his hair one more time, and headed towards the back.

The fat Elvis guy was in the corner.

"Hey, buddy, are you ready?"

"Yes, I am."

Tom followed the man into the corner before the stage. The announcer was about to begin.

"Hello, and greetings everyone," he yelled.

3.

Everybody was now waiting for Tom. Daisy stood to the far-right side of the stage. Tom was ready to go. The announcer stood in front of the stage.

"Welcome! Welcome! Are you ready for another round tonight? Tonight we have new talent coming all the way from Philadelphia! He has a new book out called 'Oriental Girls' about his sort fiction and his love for, you guessed it, Asian girls!"

Tom cracked his knuckles and swished his hair again one final time.

"Tom would like to tell you all about his observations and hypocrisies. Now please give a warm, round welcoming hand to Tom Deluge!"

All 40 people in the room clapped, including Daisy. Tom started on the stage without his glasses on, trying to look like a cool guy. He grabbed the microphone from the announcer. Tom blew into it. And he spoke.

"Hey! What's up everyone? Doing good?"

Some yells and more clapping.

"Awesome! It's good to hear that."

Tom looked on the ground for a bit. He was trying to think of something. Actually, he had some form of stage fright.

"Alright. I just want to know, how many Asian people we have in the room tonight. I want to know!"

Daisy kindly lifted her arm to show Tom's support. Two yells came from the back of the room. It looked like some Chinese girlfriend, another one on the far-left, and a lonely Asian guy.

"Not many, huh? Well, we have two girls right?"

They yelled back.

"Cool. I want to tell everyone in the room that Asian-Aryanism is a real thing. Heil or people, Heil Shinzo Abe, Heil victory!"

Tom was making fake sieg heiling. People burst out laughing. A guy actually said "hail victory!"

"Awesome. Cool beans. Well, I didn't want to talk about the coming takeover of yellow people tonight. Actually I wanted to talk about why flat chest Chinese girls give the best tit fucks ever!"

Another burst of laughs. Somewhat offensive.

Tom liked to look down at the ground like a child. He grew his hair out look so he could not make eye contact or let people see his eyes. He tried to act like an innocent kid saying naughty things.

"But no, seriously, Asian girls are better than white girls. Ummm . . . ."

A white girl made a comment from the peanut gallery.

"Fuck Asian Girls, Heil Victory!"

Tom continued.

"So, as much as it's easy to get with Asian girls, I'm going to be talking about what kind of Asian girls white guys have. It's a myth that all white guys who date Asian girls are nerdy. Okay, it may be true most of the time, but not quite."

There was a bottle of water there for Tom. He drank a bit anyway because he felt anxious.

"Okay, so any of you listen to Xiu Xiu? Anyone?"

"Hell yeah," some guy said.

"Alright, well I fan myself. And I kind of like the game. But seriously, if you want to be in a room full of queer degenerates with their Asian girlfriends, go see a Xiu Xiu show. Well, aside from the fat social justice warrior kids with the blue hair, I mean, the cool kids that go there keep it quiet. But all the cool kids . . . holy shit dude, it's Wmaffle central. Wmaffle? Know what that is? White male-Asian female."

Tom looked at that Asian guy all the way in the back.

"Not only that, but it works both ways too. So you have Asian guys going out with White girls too. It's totally real! Adrian Tomine? Ever heard of him? Good example. But seriously, every white guy in his comics got an Asian girlfriend."

Tom coughed a bit.

"So, some NPCs I saw. That is, 'Non-playable-characters," I saw. Well, first you got the one kids that has brown hair, hasn't shaved, tries to look like a Calvin Klein model, rides his bike everywhere and loves fucking video games, god, he had a fat Chinese girlfriend with fat titties and everything. Like, she's the type of girl that says she has big titties, even know they are fat and she's fucking disgusting."

He got some chuckles there."

"And she wears like big fucking cum-on-my-face Way-bearer glasses. Like, every single Asian girl has to wear those to attract a nerdy white boyfriend. Anyway, she's like a midget, kind of like Jeb Bush's wife, and this tall white kid, is fucking mute like Link from Legend of who-the-fuck-cares. You know, white kids think they are cool when they think they are a living anime character. So they pretend they are mute and say nothing. They think it's sexy when it's just fucking autistic and retarded. Also they try to look as girly as possible too."

People were laughing.

"But you have to understand that that's not everyone at the Xiu Xiu show. Those are like four kids and they all have their own Twee Asian-Aryan Facebook page and they hang out on the internet. If you ever point it out to them they have chubby Asian girls, they we will get all fucking bitchy and say they are full white girls with crossed eyes. Ching-chong, Chinky-chong!"

Tom loved to make Chinese noises to be spontaneous.

He even laughs at his own jokes.

"Haha, well. Fuck them."

More laughs from the crowd.

Daisy was clapping and laughing.

"Okay, well. They are not the only ones. Okay, so like, the cool kids, the actual cool kids, hold on, there are like, some. So let me go over them. So like, there are the big skinhead guys, ex-skinheads, who have like, really hot Chinese girlfriends. Like, elite-flat-chest-ex-porn-actress-girls. And they are like really bossy and hate other guys for not being men. And they are like the classic examples of 'we love you long time,' but they really do mean it this time. And if you ever touch one of those girls, this skinhead guy will punch you in the fucking face. Like, that's what's cool about the skinhead guys. They will stick up for their girlfriends. They will be with the guys over there, and like having a beer with one another. And then like, if a guy talks to her, he has to come in like an eagle and show dominance. These guys are the ones that do the mashing in the show. Serious nutcases."

There was silence for that part.

"And then, like, here is also another type of guy, that isn't a skinhead, but more like between an alpha and a beta, more like an 'alpha-beta,' who like, tries to at least lift weights and eat right, and dress nice. But like, they all try to act like Jamie Stewart, you know? They all get Fashcuts, all are kind of delicate and good looking, like Gore Vidal. Kind of gay or queer too, not going to lie. And then, they got like a hot Japanese girlfriend. And you're like, what the fuck dude? Like, when we say "Asian girls" we are really talking about Chinese girls. But if someone ever has a Japanese girl, they are either someone who lives on the West coast, or some very strange avant-garde shit disturber. Seriously, take a look at Yoko Ono. There is something fucking strange with Japanese gooks and their love for white guys who are queers. DING-DING-DONG WE LOVE YOU LONG TIME I LIKE GRINDCORE WES NAW!"

Again, Tom loves making Asian noises. Everyone laughs again.

"But uh . . . . Yeah. Let's talk about titties."

Everyone laughs again.

Tom was forgetting what he was originally trying to say.

"Well . . . let's see. I mean, name one time Asian girls have big tits. Japanese don't count. They are just fat and use bras to extend them or get implants. Other than, all the Asian girls I dated were flat chested or had fat ugly fish tits. I mean, again, Asian girls give the best blowjobs. Blowjob! But when you titty fucking. Serious, you just want to whack your 6 inch dick in her face instead or let her suck it. Her titties are cute, but, c'mon guys. Really? Trying to titfuck a creature that wasn't made for that? All you guys in this room have been watching paizuri porn. Tittyfucking stuff. Asian girl's just wish they could titty fuck. When really, they are only good at sucking and happy endings."

What felt like 15 minutes was only five minutes of Tom's time. He felt like he should quit any second. Still, people were laughing.

"And . . . you know. You have to ask yourself why the hell is everybody, like, wanting an Asian girlfriend."

Tom felt a little sweat coming down.

"And... So..."

He looked around. He wasn't sure what he was going to say next.

"There are these different degrees of Asian women. For starters, how do you approach one? Really all you have to do is be a white guy and hate on white women. Because white women, you know, they fucking suck. Fuck them."

Loud laughter was heard from some guys, but some boos came from some girls.

"We need to get rid of the world of white women! It's not like white men are the problem, its white women. White women have to get on their knees and start sucking dick! Like, right now. They can't stop imitating and acting like white men all the time. White men don't give a shit. They just want a good family to start, and white women don't want to do that. Now, compare that with Asian women. Asian women do a much better job being housewives. Or 'waifus' we like to call them. No one ever fucking calls a dumb blonde a fucking waifu."

"Fuck Asian people!" a loud white girl yelled.

Tom had to change the topic.

"Well, I mean . . . If white girls acted like Asians, the world would be a much better place. IF they stopped their feminist antics and pretended they were Japanese or anime characters, we would live in a much safer and happier place. White girls tonight, take notice, and start crossing your eyes and walk like a penguin. CHING-CHONG-WILLA-BING-BONG!"

The audience found it funny when Tom made racial remarks equally about everyone. Yet Tom was trying to focus and persuade the audience that Asian girls were actually better.

"No offense, but it's true," Tom awkwardly said.

He was looking around in the audience. Good thing he didn't have his glasses on.

"Well, has like, anyone seen like, any cartoon show on the TV? Like, *Steven Universe* or *Star vs. The Forces of Evil*? Seriously. Like if you take a look at anyone in the show, it's usually a white guy dating an Asian or everyone is half Asian. Fuck. That is something that is happening now a television. I think it's a West Coast thing, so I blame everyone in California for allowing to happen."

"White Power!" yelled a man in the back.

"And . . . like . . . I really don't like video games, but you Asian girls, most white guys don't like video games so stop pretending that you should like video games too, to woo over a white guy. Most white men I know, they want to be strong. All you have to do is approach them and say you're interested and any strong guy will be all over you.

That easy. You know, Fuck Mega Man, fuck Capcom, fuck Street Fighter, fuck every single SWPL, American, 80's nostalgic, faggot in this room because that is fucking pussy shit!"

Everybody was laughing.

"Do some race-play once in awhile. Call your boyfriend a cracker. Call him a KKK white supremacist, I don't care. So as long we can call you a fucking dumb chink that can't drive a car."

The laughing soon turned to applauding.

"Trust me. Sex becomes amazing. Sex is so amazing when you start fucking your girlfriend in the ass and call her a bug-looking tiger mom with a sideways vagina. And girls, we like it when you say you want to be dominated by our huge racist white cocks that just turns on everyone."

The lewd behavior seemed to out of control.

"But uhhh . . . yeah. My advice for guys trying to get with Asian girls? Stay in school, get a Master's degree, stay clean-cut, eat healthy, exercise daily, fucking shave, stand up right, wear the right clothes, go to places when she is asking for you, and all that fun. It really is to do these kind of things."

Tom searched the room for the merchant table. He pointed his finger towards there.

"My book is over there, please support me and follow me on YouTube, all that fun stuff! Thank you so much guys!"

Tom bowed liked an obedient Asian. Like he was doing a shinto prayer.

Claps and some roars came from the crowd. Tom nodded his head to the manager. The announcer came over to take his mic. Tom waved to everyone and went back stage. The announcer said, "Tom Deluge everyone!"

It felt like only half the audience was clapping this time than the full audience when he first got up on stage.

"Up next we got another comedian who was once a football quarterback for the Minnesota Vikings. Stay tuned!"

Tom blanked out. He could have joked for another 10 minutes, but completely forgot what he was even trying to say to the audience. Half of what he was trying to say got out. But he completely forgot when he was in the moment. Hopefully, Tom could be consider the Andy Kaufman of Asian-American comedy. Maybe. If they let him sly with his bad performance.

After the clapping, Tom stood behind the stage. He let out a big long sigh. The show was over. Daisy came over to pat him on the back. Tom was a little startled.

"You did great!" she said.

"You think so? I thought it was okay."

"Whatever, put it behind you now. You tried." She smiled.

Both Tom and Daisy took a seat in the background to relax. The manager approached Tom.

"Good show kid. You're funny, like always."

"Thanks."

Tom stretched his back. He looked back at Daisy. "She would even bother about staying here?"

Daisy looked around. She saw the ugly Santa-Claus-looking-man sleeping on the floor.

"Yeah, let's get out of here. We know what this place is all about now."

"You're right."

Tom got up to give all his newly made friends a goodbye.

Still, there was no sign of Jake that night. Both of them had to move on without him.

4.

Outside the venue, Daisy took to the front on the car. She was going to drive. Before he got in, Tom had to take a piss behind the building. He didn't feel like going back inside and using the toilet. The place is a dump anyway.

Tom slid in the front seat. "Thanks for driving this time. I'm beat."

"You piss in the corner like some kind of dog."

"Oh, whatever. Who cares? Where are we supposed to go?"

Daisy messed with the GPS beforehand.

"Let's stop at the Hampton Hotel. It's about five minutes away."

"Awesome. I'm so tired."

Daisy set the car in drive. They were on their way. Tom looked back at the Rodman place. A strange little place it was. They gave it a shot. He wasn't sure if he would ever go back there again.

The car was set in motion. Tom had sweat up a storm. He drank too much water after the show. He was in a post-anxiety phase.

The radio played a very familiar song. There was wacky sounding synthesizer in the intro.

Tom, half tired, recognized the beat. "Hey, I know what this is . . . this song."

The loud chugging guitar was very nostalgic.

"It was in that movie. The movie with those zombies. A while back."

Daisy butted in, "*28 Days Later.*"

"Yes! The part where they go food shopping!" Tom said with laughter.

"This is such a good song," she said, as she turned up the radio. Daisy continued, "You know, that place we were at, really felt like some kind of 28 Days Later. They were all zombies and kind of felt like we were in a post-apocalyptic shelter."

Tom clapped his hands.

"Yes! That is so true! We actually survived that! This song is prophetic!"

Both were laughing as the song about zombies played on.

They were only a few minutes away from the hotel. Tom noticed a book in the car he never saw before. It was most likely Daisy's. He lifted it from the ground and expected the book.

Floating, Brilliant, Gone by Franny Choi.

"What is this?" Tom asked.

"Oh, it's another book of poetry. AKA word art. Silly stuff."

Tom skimmed through the pages. He looked at the pretty illustrations.

"Wait, I think who this. Is this the girl, that . . . ."

As Tom was about to continue and finish his sentence, Daisy nodded her head up and down, and said, "Yep, it's her. Ms. Sit Down and Let Us Abolish You."

"Yes! I knew it was her! When did you get this book?"

"I just got the book before and brought it along to read. It's pretty good!"

Tom was skimming through the pages.

"And Richard Spencer basically gave her free publicity at American Renaissance. Funny shit."

Tom read some of Choi's lines.

"This stuff is actually good. Do you think she really means what she says, or just looking for attention?"

"I think she's totally PC and doesn't know what she wants. But I think we would be totally awesome girlfriends if we met."

Tom had a smile on his face.

"When she says, 'Sit Down and let me abolish you,' it sounds like, she wants some of that white cock."

Daisy turned her head.

"What!?"

"Nothing."

Tom was being mischievous. He chuckled.

"I think she really is one of us," he said.

Daisy was laughing.

"I bet she has a white boyfriend too."

"No, like, she does. You don't need to prove it. She's acting like a feminist so she can get herself a nice white husband. I can do a pretty good impersonation for her."

Tom started to talk like a high-pitch-valley-girl with a tiger mom accent.

"Hi, guys! It's me! Mandy Wong! I love white boys and I think racism is bad! Oh my god! I fucking love MGMT!"

Daisy was laughing.

"I heard you do that before! That's um . . . You did a video on that!"

"Yes! I did! Everyone on the Hapa subreddit gets pissed off when I am her."

"Wait, is Mandy just you pretending to be like . . . ."

"I guess so!" Tom laughed aloud.

"That is so funny!" she said.

"I fucking love Franny and everything she does. I wish more people were like her!" Tom said.

The GPS yelled out, "turn-right-on-Henderson-towards-final-destination, on-right."

They were here at the hotel.

Daisy had to find a parking spot.

"Let's reserve one night only."

"Okay."

Able to find their spot, both got out of the car, got their belongings, and headed for the hotel clerk. The long day is almost coming to an end.

Daisy successfully rented a room overnight. She put it on her credit card. Obviously her parents had the money for that kind of thing. They were assigned the 5th floor, Room 213. Tom and Daisy just had their backpacks.

Tom had to stop at the refreshment booth for some free cupcakes. He took a bite out of one. Meanwhile, Daisy took a large can of whip cream.

"Let's go," Tom said in a tired voice. Both headed down the hall and went inside the elevator. Alone in the elevator, Daisy had to something giddy.

"The clerk was another lazy Mexican."

"Yo, what's up with Arizona and all these dirty Mexicans?"

"I think they get the jobs nobody else wants to do."

"Once the wall is built, all of them are going back home," Tom said snidely.

Getting out of the elevator, Tom looked both ways down the hall, realizing 201 starts to the left. Walling over to their room, Tom looked back at Daisy. She wasn't there. Looking up, Tom was in for a surprise. Daisy squirted the can of whip cream onto his face. He jumped back a bit. Daisy laughed aloud.

"Ahh! What the hell was that for!?"

"I found it on the booth and thought it would be funny to use it!" She smiled.

Daisy was a bigger prankster than Tom was. He didn't get mad at her. She was a cute girl. She loved him so much that she would play such a prank on him.

Daisy squirted some more whip cream on Tom's shirt as he backed up. Like if it was a gun of freeze tag. Tom started to laugh.

"I should fucking kill you."

"You sound like that one video with the fat kid that gets shot by fucking paintballs."

Tom found room 213. He slide the card-key into the door. Enough with this already!

"Don't wake the fucking neighbors. It's quiet hours!"

"Oh, shit! Somebody is getting mad!" Daisy teased.

Luckily they got in their room before they can make any more noise outside.

Inside, they had two beds, a TV, a fridge, a bathroom, and an outside porch. Daisy dropped her bags. She laid on the bed first. "Who's going to take a shower first?"

"I should. I got cum shot on by whip cream."

Daisy laughed.

Tom put his bag down, and went in the bathroom to undress.

"I wonder if this TV has video games on it. Like super Nintendo or GameCube games. Back then I did. I remember when my family took me to Miami and they had things like those," she said.

Tom, in the bathroom, yelled back, "Oh, yeah, and Diddy Kong Country. I bought it because I felt like it and my dad got pissed off at me because it was $15 or something. I didn't know what I was doing in the game. It was like this pirate ship and stuff."

"This totally reminds me of my family vacation."

Daisy opened the porch windows. The traffic of the cars can be heard. Lights visible of the city could be seen. It was dark and windy on a perfect sunny night.

"I love tonight! I love the fresh air. It's so nice! I'm so glad we went out!"

"Me too," Tom said from a distance. "Taking a shower," he continued.

Tom hopped in the shower to rinse himself off. Daisy did some unpacking and a little texting.

Tom rinsed off in the shower. Looking at his stomach, it was a little fat. Though he was fit, he always looked at his body as being ugly. Shampooing his hair, his mind worked liked a checklist. Next, he had to get up in the morning and go to Santa Barbara. That was his next destination. He had to watch out for alerts from Jake. That would be nice. And then maybe he could finally talk about getting a book deal with him. Either revising Oriental Girls or creating a new book. He didn't have any ideas for a new one. Oriental Girls was fine already. Taking a hot shower sure made him feel less anxious.

After the shower, Tom grabbed a towel, and washed off. There was a knock on the bathroom door. Tom always had the towel over his nipples like he was a girl. As he opened the door, he was surprised to find a naked Daisy. Her tits stood out like daggers. She was almost flat chested.

"It's my turn to take a shower now!" she said like a little kid. Tom was shocked to see Daisy naked in front of him. Blood rushed through his penis.

"Stripping naked all of a sudden and I didn't get out of the shower!" he said.

"You look like a little bitch when you wear a towel like that!" Again, teasing him like she was a little kid. And the way she said it too. She sounded liked an 8 year old.

"Get out of here!" Tom said.

Daisy pranced into the small bathroom with her naked body. Tom had his shoulder against her naked tit.

That's a reason why Tom loves Daisy. Totally unpredictable.

Tom got into his skimpy white shirt and shorts as pajamas. He looked out on the back porch. He felt refreshed. Tonight was a good night.

Tom turned on the TV and tucked himself in one bed. He was so tired. He felt grateful to be in a cozy bed. Now he felt like he was a little kid again.

After Daisy's shower, she went and put her pajamas on in front of Tom.

"Ha, look, this is so funny. They are not playing *CatDog* at 9 o'clock. I have good memories of old Nickelodeon cartoon shows."

"I never watched cartoons," Daisy said while putting on her shorts.

"Well, there was a lot of good ones. I have this one particular memory of watching Kablam before bed in a hotel like this. Kablam had this one short called 'The Prometheus and Bob Tapes.' I thought it was the coolest show ever. That night, however, I had a nightmare about the scary UFO and Camerabot that are shown in the beginning of the show."

Daisy tucked herself into the other bed.

"That's why you don't watch cartoons before bed. You'll get nightmares!"

Tom put on CatDog. It was an episode starring them in a cave and fighting over rock candy.

"You're 24 and you still watch cartoons?"

"Yes, yes, I do," Tom replied.

"What else is on?"

"Let me see . . . ."

The only channels that Tom ever desired to watch were cartoons and NHK. He hated reruns of decade old movies and boring shows. Tom tuned onto Nascar.

"Look! Race cars!"

"How can anyone watch cars go round and round in circles and find it entertaining?"

Tom thought about that before it. He changed the channel again.

"What do you like?"

"How about you put on the news?"

Tom surfed the channels.

"RT or CNN?"

"Either one."

"Fuck RT," Tom said.

The news had something about Trump on it.

"I like how calming the news is at night. I like the words scrolling down at the screen and the murmuring of the voices," she said.

"The new is only interesting when the world is going to blow up or when Trump does something cool," Tom said.

Tom took a deep breath. He was getting tired.

He and Daisy talked for some bit about personal matters and the strange people they saw today. Tom often worried whether his skit was good or just plain bad. Either way, it was done. Tom didn't have to do another unless Jake plans one. He hasn't been on Discord yet to talk to Jake again. He didn't feel like opening up his computer. Maybe he should start writing a new book of material then relying on his improvisations. Oriental Girls is where he had something to say.

After two hours of talking, Tom and Daisy were ready to go to bed.

"Daisy, do you think what I am doing is good?"

"Of course it is. Don't stress yourself out. I love what you're doing too!"

"I get stressed before bed. Ever since I was a kid, I would tell my mom I would get the 'Ws' or worries before bed. And I would question whatever if I would live the next day. I was super suicidal, but I didn't know what suicide was or how to even kill myself."

"That sounds so funny. Why would you try and kill yourself?"

"I don't want to kill myself. That is, I just wanted to feel dreadful depression and do nothing. I don't have to urge to kill myself. More like, how I dealt was anxiety, was being in a certain motion over and over again. I really don't know how to explain it."

"Everything is okay, babe," Daisy said.

"Alright," Tom taking in another deep breath. He turned off the TV and turned off the light.

"Goodnight, Daisy. I love you."

"I love you. Goodnight, Tom," she said, while she cuddled herself on her side of the bed.

…Not like tonight they were in the same bed. Tom felt he had some more room for leg space. Sleeping in the same bed requires leg space and respect for one's area.

The city lights glared across the ceiling. Tom was looking straight up at it. Always in hotel rooms there was this glare from the outside traffic. The rushing noises of cars could be heard all night long. It wasn't a pitch black darkness in a forest. Tom was alone in his thoughts again. Things felt okay. His girl wished him a goodnight. He talked to strangers today. Nobody was after him. He could finally fall asleep in a position of security.

But like always, Tom had trauma that haunted him. His dreams were always strange.

5.

Tom would fall asleep thinking about the good things in life, like his favorite board games, like Cosmic Encounter and Cosmic Wimpout. Or even think about casual sex with Daisy. How grateful he was to have her. Most people didn't have girlfriends. Or, at least that was what he thought. Tom still had trauma from his college years. It's only been a year since he has been out of college, and such much he has done since then, he should have done before he even entered college. If only he was in a secure position and not having to suffer through his mundane student schedule. He didn't meet friends at that time. He studied what he wanted to do.

Thinking about school made Tom anxious. The thought of Daisy was much more pleasant. Eventually, moving around and thinking of her, he would go to sleep.

But every night, for some time now, Tom had been receiving prophetic or lucid dreams. The same characters reappeared in his dreams. Incarnations of those characters he met in college.

The devils that would haunt him in his sleep were Jack and Sarah.

Tom dreamed that he was in school again. This time, school was out in the middle of a cornfield. Outside, there was a long reaching road from left to right that never ended. Sort of like the gas station he was at earlier today. Tom was locked in the building. There was no way to get out.

Up front, there was a store clerk that looked like an old teacher he knew. She said to him, "Your class is about to begin. Go down that hall and I will sign you in."

As if this was a job in his dream. Tom walked in the other room, the other half of the building, and he saw grown-up young adults playing like little kids in kindergarten. Everyone was playing on the ground. Tom was the only one standing. In these lucid dreams, Tom would observe and walk around like it was an art museum.

Sarah, the girl that always haunted him, sat in a desk and read something off her laptop. That laptop with the Pikachu and Mega Man sticker that would haunt him. Tom saw her from all angles. She stood there like a frozen mannequin. Tom also spotted a bunch of mutated kids playing a game of Killer Bunnies on the ground. A silly card game that he grew up with. Tom found an exit door behind him. It lead him into another overwhelming room. There was no students in this room, but it was some library replaced with every single Sega Genesis game ever made. There was another lazy clerk reading a book at the desk.

The video games were held on library shelfs, like a perfect achieve. You could take these games out at any time and play them. On the shelf, Tom read a big book size copy of "Sonic & Knuckles." Other games like "The Ooze" and "Comix Zone" were there. The size of these games were as big as outdated encyclopedias. Tom looked at them with awe. Games like these brought back his earliest memories doing nothing as a toddler. He wanted to find a way out of this labyrinth. Suddenly, music started to play over the telecom. The Legend of Zelda theme song. Tom hated the game. He never played it, but knew of it because it is often associated in "gamer" culture. The song was so cringe worthy, Tom ran out of the room, finding a door. The door lead back into the first room. Another school clerk looked at him. The old teacher told him to go back into the school room. Tom was going in a big circle. Back into the original school room, all the students were huddled around a circle like some kind of satanic ritual. Rather, they were playing a large game of Red Dragon INN, a rip-off of an already popular board game, Cosmic Encounter (one of Tom's favorite). It looked like about 40 people were playing a single game of Red Dragon INN. Tom peeped over the crowd. He could not tell what was going on. Jack and Sarah were sitting together. Jack turned his head like an exorcist child.

"Come over here Tom and come sit with us!"

Tom resisted the urge to sit with them, even though Jack came off as a nice person. A possessive trauma was controlling Tom. Tom again had to run out of the room.

What he thought was the original room he came in from, then became a long hallway of windows. Windows that looked outside a desolate cornfield. The hallway curved into another large play room. A room which was called, "The Jungle Palace." A large arcade with three floors was now a part of this school. Tom now had to do something . . . something he forgot. His legs moved over to a place he didn't want to go. Again, he was going up stairs that would descend. And somehow Jack was there again, walking pass him with ease. Jack smiled at Tom. Tom horrified. Behind him followed Suzy, a sexy and hot Chinese girl. Tom knew who Suzy was, a non-existent character who had always existed within his unconsciousness. Both Jack and Suzy were able to make it up the stairs. Tom, now running, still remained in the same place. The girl Sarah was already up the stairs. Jack and Suzy joined her. Before the three left, the stairs let Tom make it up the stairs. In his dream, he was sweating. Jack, Suzy, and Sarah, already in the middle of a game of Magic: The Gathering. Only under 15 seconds. Time and Space in Tom's dream was distorted. Jack looked upset. Jack, who was friendly towards Tom, now was cold. Tom started to burst out in tears, and run down the stairs again, into a black hole. His emotions were being manipulated. Tom did not know where he was going. His dream was flying by him without any reason. Jack and Sarah has always messed with his sleep. The first day he met Jack in his sleep was a year ago. A tea room with dead bodies on the ground. And he talked like such a gentlemen. And tonight, Jack was hacking into Tom's sleep again. How could he?

…Tom woke up.

He felt like a hammer was pounding on his head. He hadn't drunk any alcohol in the past hours. His room was still dark. The light ran above the ceiling. Too tired to check the time, Tom assumed it was four in the morning. Breathing deeply, everything was fine. Daisy was in a deep sleep in the other bed. Everything is okay. Well, not really.

It felt like the whole situation was real. It felt like that did actually happen. Was it a chemical imbalance in his body that made him feel this way? He wasn't so sure. Or was it a college trauma he could never overcome? That feeling like he didn't belong anywhere. He was alone in his hotel room in the dark.

Tom got up from his bed and looked outside on the back porch. The city lights were still on and the cars going there on way. Nothing changed in the early morning. There was no use sitting outside. The best thing to do was to go back to bed. His head still ached. The memories of college came back to him. The feeling of being bullied was so harsh. But it was all over. He had to put the past behind him and move on.

Tom closed his eyes. He thought about Daisy. How grateful he was at that moment in time. The suffering was worth it.

Daisy got up at 9:30. She was boiling green tea on the stove. Tom woke as well. His eyes were open. He was looking at her. Thirty minutes later, he turned over on his bed like he was a dog.

"Do you want some tea?" she asked.

"Maaaaahhhhhh," said Tom, like if he was a Gremlin.

Both did their morning routines to get up. It took him an hour to get ready for the day. As they were talking, Tom had today's plans.

"Let's go to Santa Barbara and meet up with Jake," he said.

"Aren't we going to meet up with your other friend? That radio host?"

Tom thought about what she was trying to say.

"You mean Howard? Oh, yeah, he lives in Santa Barbara. We are definitely going to meet up with him. I will shoot him a text."

Jake and Howard. Two people that they will hopefully meet tonight. One or the other.

"Alright, I will drive this time, I think I am okay."

"Did you have bad dreams last night? I heard you were up last night."

It was true. Tom did have another nightmare.

At least Daisy understood Tom's trauma.

"Yeah, I did. It was not that bad."

"Did it have something to do with that girl again?"

"Yeah, it did. She was in my dreams again. I can't shake her off. I don't know."

Daisy put her arms around his back.

"It's okay, Tom. Don't think about it. I have trauma too. It's ok."

She smiled at Tom.

Tom smiled back. Everything was okay.

"Alright, let's go see Jake tonight!" Tom sounding optimistic.

Tom and Daisy packed their bags to get ready. Before Daisy turned off the TV she asked, "Tom, did you want finish watching Right Now Kapow?"

Tom laughed.

"No thanks, let's go."

She turned off the TV. They went down the hallway and into the escalator. They checked out and headed outside to the car.

This is where things got too strange.

Heading for the car, a girl with blonde hair approached both of them. She was Asian looking. Maybe Japanese with a blonde wig.

"Excuse me, Sir. Are you Tom?"

Tom looked at her. "Yes, I am."

Daisy looked at Tom. Tom didn't know who this mysterious girl approaching him was.

This girl asked, "Are you heading to meet up with Jake?"

"Yes, how did you know?" he asked.

The girl looked at him. "My name is Nancy. I am Jake's girlfriend."

Tom now remembered what the name "Nancy" was all about. "Nancy" was spoken many times by Jake. There was also potential that Jake and Nancy would meet again.

This was all too sudden.

Nancy spoke to Tom, "I came to chase after you guys. You were at Rodman's last night. I asked one of the guys and they said you were here."

Daisy was a little scared. This girl was a total stalker.

"Wow, well, it's nice to meet you," Tom said.

"I need to come along with you guys," she suddenly said.

"Do you have a car? " Daisy said.

Nancy, with a cold face, "I took an Uber to see you guys."

This girl was desperate.

"Well, I mean, you're welcome to come along," Tom said without thinking about it.

Daisy wasn't sure to trust her.

"We have to meet up with Jake. I'm excited to see him. But more importantly, I know someone else you might know."

Tom looked back at her. "Who might that be?"

"Suzy," she said.

Suzy. The girl that was in his dream last night.

Tom was shocked. How did this girl know about his dreams?

"Suzy? Suzy who?"

"The girl that teases you in your sleep," Nancy said with a smile.

Daisy was shocked.

What was going on?

"Let's go see Jake and then we can meet up with Suzy as well."

Tom interrupted her.

"Woah, wait. How do you know this?"

"Know what?"

"My dreams?"

"Your dreams?"

"Yeah like, how the hell do you know about it?"

Nancy looked at him.

"I don't know what you're talking about."

"My dreams! Suzy is a character in my sleep!"

Tom felt like now he was talking to himself. Why would a stranger know what he was talking about?

Nancy, with her cold dead face, looked at both Tom and Daisy.

"We are going to be good friends. Trust me guys, I am really good friends with Jake."

Tom had no choice to bring her along for the ride and interrogate her as they drove to California.

"Alright," Tom said. "But do you have any money on you in case we need it?"

"Sure. I have it," she said.

"Dude, how do you know about Suzy," Daisy said in an agitated tone.

"Suzy was a girl that hanged around Villanova. The same college Tom went to. We were friends for a bit. I heard of Tom through Jake and what Tom has been doing on the road. It's nice to meet you guys. Sorry for being so confrontational," Nancy said.

Tom headed for the car. Daisy and Nancy followed.

"Did you go to Villanova?" Tom said.

"No, not really. I hanged out with friends there. It wasn't my scene. Too snobby," she replied.

Tom and Daisy had to take in a stranger on for a ride with them. She seemed kind of nice. She looked like a Japanese android. Daisy was still skeptical.

"Why didn't you just meet up with Jake then?" Daisy said.

"I wanted to see Tom perform at Rodman's last night. I couldn't make it. I was in a different state. It is more important that I see you guys in person before I go ahead and meet Jake for the first time."

"Wait, for the first time?" Tom said as he was getting into the driver's seat.

"We are good internet friends. We Skype quite a bit. But, I am going to meet him for the first time. Just like you guys are," she said.

Tom, Daisy, and Nancy were all going to meet Jake for the first time.

"No way," Tom said.

"Yeah. We are totally internet boyfriend and girlfriend."

Every moment was getting more weirder.

"Do you meet him on like, Facebook, or . . . ?"

"We met on a dating website. Then everything else followed. We are all going to meet him IRL, how's about that guys?"

This time, Nancy sounded a little cheerful. Odd. Since this is coming from a dead looking person.

Tom and Daisy felt odd about the situation. They could not talk in the corner and make a final judgement. They had to go on this adventure. Bringing along another person on the trip was convenient. At least she had money.

Daisy sat up in the front seat. Nancy pressed herself in the back. There was enough room. She was messing with her hair.

Tom had to ask her.

"Is that a wig?"

Nancy looked back. "Yes, it is. I love blonde hair. I want hair like this."

6.

Once on the highway, Tom focused on driving, while Daisy and Nancy talked to one another.

They were going to be on the road for a good four hours. They should be in Santa Barbara around 3 PM.

Nancy was enough entertainment for the both of them.

The road to California was one long straight line, with other strangers on the road.

"Jake would text me daily like I was his teddy bear. I would always answer back. We didn't start Skyping until a few months later. And then two years later, we are finally going to meet each other," Nancy said.

Tom felt disgruntled.

"Did you ever sext online?" he said. Daisy laughed.

"Umm, yeah, we did. Why?" Nancy said unapologetically.

"It sounds like Jake really has a bad case of autism and he's so desperate to talk to a good-looking stranger every day when he is upset with the world."

"I don't think he's autistic. He works out once a week and is quite handsome, have you seen him?"

Tom recalled the Skype sessions he had with Jake and his voice. The two things didn't add up with Nancy's picture.

"No, not really."

"I met Tom online too," Daisy butted in. "The difference was, we were so close to one another. I was only two cities away from him."

"I guess you're right about distance. I was crazy enough to call someone all the way from New Jersey. New Jersey is a hellhole. Nothing happens there. Everyone is miserable and depressed. The place looks like you're lost in an endless forest. Everyone was a creep too. There is seriously no Asian community there."

Daisy giggled.

"Really? I knew a Chinese friend from Trenton."

"No, it's not like that at all. Try being the only pretty Japanese there. I would always have to go out of my way and hang around Edgewater or New York to get away from it all."

"A Japanese with a wig, huh? You might as well be white then," Tom said.

Nancy laughed.

"I like being white, thank you. I wish I had blonde hair and wish I had a nice white boyfriend. Everyone in Jersey is judgmental. Strangers will sometimes call me chink and I hate it."

"Don't you think your taking that too seriously? And rather somebody just said 'chink' and it's not just you?" rebutted Tom.

"I like being Japanese. I like white culture more."

"That kind of sounds like Asian-Aryanism, does it, Tom?" Daisy spoke over to him, like if it was a joke.

Tom took the concept of Asian-Aryanism seriously.

"I mean," Tom said was focusing on the wheel. "I can see where you're coming from. But, are you some kind of yellow feminist?"

"A what?"

"A feminist."

"No, what did you say before?"

"A yellow feminist. Do you know what that is?"

"Not really."

"Okay, it's like, a normal feminist is a white girl that wants equality between the sexes of white male and white female. But when feminism is translated in Eastern culture, it adapts Confucian values. So when Asian girls get into feminism, they want to break their traditions by finding themselves a white husband, which in return advocates the very 'patriarchy' thing that white girls hate."

Nancy thought about it for a second.

"Uhh . . . what?"

"Long story short, white girls fucking suck and Asian girls are much better," Tom said with a smile.

"It's like there is this whole anti-white agenda within feminism, but when feminism tries to translate with other

Asians, they see it as an opportunity to be Americanized," Daisy was trying to explain to Nancy.

"I think I know where you guys are coming from now. Well, no, I don't hate white people."

Tom felt a little hostile.

"So do you want white cock or not?"

Nancy smiled, "Hell yeah!"

Everyone laughed.

"I didn't think you could have any advance form of racism like that. I think it's okay for anyone wanting to belong to one race or another. ...I'm quite surprise Tom you would be more of a guy that is all for 'weeb nationalism' and Asian girls rule stuff. I don't see what's so special with Asian girls."

That comment ticked Tom off.

"Funny, that's coming from an Asian girl and Daisy, who is my girlfriend, is right there too. It's a white guy thing. Do I ever question why you like white cock? No. Then that must be an Asian girl thing."

Daisy was laughing.

"Well what makes it even more strange is Nancy is Japanese and I am Chinese. So shouldn't we be all at each other's throats?" she said.

Nancy was amused. "Really? I thought you looked like you were Filipino or something?"

"What!?" Daisy said. "No, I am Chinese!"

"That is really funny," Nancy said as a simple thought.

"Then it must be a Chinese thing that Chinese girls like White guys and it must be a Japanese thing for Japanese girls to want to be like white people," Tom said.

Nancy thought about it.

"I guess you're right. I had one another Japanese friend, and she had an American name too, and was all into white people stuff. Like plaid shirts and rock music."

Tom started laughing.

"Stuff White People Like by Christian Lander? That is such a good book!"

Nancy laughed. "Oh, haha. No, I never read that book."

"White people are unique and we have our own identity. Let's see, for starters, we like punk rocks shows, and vegan restaurants, and nerd conventions, and most importantly, Asian girls!"

Daisy burst out laughing.

"It's true!" he said.

"Then why are white people not open about these things?" Nancy said.

"Because white people are cucked everyday with cultural Marxist propaganda and something innate in their nature wants to be quiet about their own racial identity. Or I think they are just not allowed to open about being racial," he said.

"Wait . . . what? This sounds like a conspiracy. I like the part in your book where you say Whites and Asians should get together to form their own Asian-Aryan race, but about white people... don't white people know about this?"

"Are you kidding me? White people think Asian-Aryanism is an advanced form of racism and the norm doesn't question of much of the opposite it really is. Nobody on the far-right, far-left, or far-norm doesn't understand Asian-Aryanism!"

"Why not?"

"Because white people are committing white genocide and would rather be left alone to their own radical centralism!"

Nancy thought about it for a bit.

"This is some deep stuff. I didn't know your own philosophy went this far!" she said.

"It's pretty easy to understand. White people don't think in terms of their own racial consciousness, they are cucked from other non-whites, mostly Asians, and they will have half-kids and be all like, 'my son is white or has universal values, so he's one citizen of the human race,' and that bullshit."

"It's super easy to understand," Daisy said.

"I know what you guys are saying," Nancy said.

"Then?"

Nancy was thinking.

"Why aren't they open about it?"

Tom rolled his eyes.

"You have to understand the whole alt-right phenomena and must address that we are in a post-multicultural-diversity era. The egalitarian ideology will not lose another century. Only black use it for 'gibsmedat' and we live in what I like to call, 'a liberal feudalist society.' Whites are slowly waking up to nationalism, and it's only a matter of time before white guys with their Asian girlfriends, and hopefully vice versa too, will become racially motivated and work for the interested of their half children and society."

Nancy thought about.

"That sounds dope. I like that."

"And I think you a perfect Asian-Aryan woman, I think you need to be yellow-pilled though."

"Ha, what? Yellow-pilled?"

"Yeah, it's like being red-pilled, but instead you know Asian society is the truth . . . or that white cock is the truth!"

Nancy was laughing. "So I am yellow-pilled?"

"Pretty much, you have to open about it and tell others that white guys are the truth for Asian women. The same I am telling white guys that Asian women are the truth. And as well telling Asian guys that white girls are truthful too. Especially weeb white girls."

"Wait, but what about like, Asian guys?"

"Asian guys are fine. There is this whole hapa scene on the internet that claims they are victims and should be social justice warriors, but that's not the truth of it. Most normal Asian guys just want to be white guys. The same with every single hapa guy. They don't have any guidance or direction. They get racially confused and become retards. I think the far-right love the hapa argument because it tells whites to stick with their own kind, and as well as the Asians."

"It's like, I don't see that much Asian male, White female relationships going on that much."

"Because it's not popular and not developed enough to have the words and meaning. White guys go out with Asian girls because it is popular to do so. Any male figure will always have dominate influence. Once Asian males or Hapa males get powerful, Asian male White female will become a thing. Give it time. If you want to solve the weakness of the hapa or Asian male, I suggest every one of them should read Yukio Mishima or even don Yaoi aesthetics."

"Ahh, that is totally interesting," thought Nancy.

And so they had a long dialogue about Asian-Aryanism in the car. Tom and Daisy learned more about Nancy. She wasn't an evil person like they imagined her to be. They got swept up in the conversations about white and Asian race relations, internet humor, personal life, and art they liked.

Getting tired out, Nancy and Daisy took a nap. Tom was only a few miles towards Santa Barbara. He had the exact GPS location where Jake lived.

In California, Tom had to make a pit stop to get some food and drink. Again, it was another 711.

As Tom entered the store, he spot a white male, Asian female couple leaving the store. Was Jake right about California being a central for Asian-Aryanism? Should h move from his local Philadelphia all the way to California? Doe he even have the money to pay for it?

The cashier was also a Chinese. Odd.

Tom left the store with a Monster, Cheese Slim Jims, and three hot-dogs.

Back in the car, he gave the hotdogs to Daisy and Nancy. Tom ate his Slim Jim in the car before he took on the hotdog. That strange feeling where eating lunch in the car feels dirty and claustrophobic.

"You know, I just saw a White male / Asian female couple walk out of the 711. Nancy, have you ever been to California?"

Nancy was opening the ketchup packet for her hotdog. "Nope, this is my first time!"

I think it's a really beautiful city. I love all the palm trees. Maybe we should consider moving here Tom!" Daisy said.

She read his mind. California is a nice place to live. Could both of them afford living here if they had the money?

"Not only is that it's nice. I am now starting to believe that Asian-Aryanism is real and white people have been practicing it for over40 years now. They just have been quiet about it because it's their like, natural white people instinct to be quiet about things," Tom said.

"They are quiet about a lot of things," Nancy observed.

There was one thing though that Tom had to ask Nancy about. They were having fun talking about whatever in the

66

car, but the thought about Suzy disturbed him. What did Nancy know about Suzy? Does Nancy know about Tom's trauma?

After Tom finished his Slim Jim, he had to ask her.

"So, what do you meet Suzy?"

"Suzy?"

"Yeah, Suzy."

"What about her?"

"You know about my dreams, right?"

"Not really. I say I do, but I am just reading from your blog post. She's a character in your sleep that haunts you?"

"Yeah."

Tom thought about it for a bit.

"The Suzy in my dream has black hair and a red dress, and you're telling me the same Suzy you know has that too?"

"Yeah. Isn't that a coincidence?"

Nancy took a bite from her hotdog.

"Tom has college trauma. I totally understand where he is coming from," Daisy said.

"What happened?" Nancy asked.

Tom looked down. The story of his past was very personal.

"Um . . . It's a long story. It's long. But, basically, I was bullied and I was hated for being cis-white male in college."

"Hah, that doesn't sound so bad," Nancy said.

Tom got mad.

"You don't understand. You don't know what it's like to be a class clown or loser. A position everyone wants you to be and you don't want to fulfil. Against my will."

Nancy quickly understood.

"I see. Let's not talk about it then."

"But no. I find it strange, is that you know a Suzy you hanged out with. What was college like for you?"

Nancy thought about it.

"I didn't graduate. I recently dropped out. Too much money and boring. I may reconsider in the future and transfer somewhere. I had fun."

Tom looked a little upset. He had something against popular girls and their behavior. He saw that through Nancy.

"My college time was much worse," Daisy interrupted.

"I was at a private girl's school with no boys. And all the girls were pretty much spoiled brats and wannabe lesbians. I don't think none of them knew what a lesbian was. All of them were white girls trying to be intellectually pretentious. I was seriously the only Chinese on my campus. I hate feminist and I hate when girls dominate. They are pathetic."

Daisy told her story to Tom when they first met. Tom could understand where she was coming from.

Nancy continued, "Well, for me. I had a guy friend into hardcore. He was ok. I dumped him later on. The scene at Villanova was so inauthentic. Fart boys and Christian conservative everywhere. You had to go to the city if you

wanted to have fun. The classrooms were really boring. I
didn't like the scene at all. I met Suzy in class."

Nancy paused for a bit.

"Suzy knew a guy named Jack, who really into The
Hoedown Truth, the podcast you do Tom."

Jack.

Was it the same Jack in his dream?

"Jack? Jack who?" Tom was getting agitated.

"I don't remember his last name. All I knew her friend
was Jack. They were into geeky stuff like board games and
stuff like that."

Those two topics in one sentence triggered Tom. This
had to be a coincidence. Feeling nervous, he did not want
to bring up Jack from his sleep. Jack, the ghoul that would
haunt him in his sleep.

"Well, my college life was shitty."

"Same," Nancy said.

Everyone in the car remained silent as they hate their
hotdogs. The radio was still playing Nigger-tunes.

7.

Ten minutes later they were back on the highway.Daisy was content looking out the window, as the breeze hit her face. Tom received a text from Jake earlier. Tom wrote,

"We are on our way."

"Great. At my house," Jake wrote back.

Tom was a little upset thinking about Jack and Suzy. Those names he never wants he hear again. Daisy changed the subject to something charming.

"California is beautiful. The weather is so nice. I wish we had a house here," Daisy said.

"It reminds me of Japan when I think about it. I was there for only a few weeks when I was 15. Tokyo had a mix of White and Japanese people," Nancy added.

"Really? Do you California tries and emulate Japan?"

"From what I am observing, I think it does."

Tom had to say something funny.

"Minus all the blonde, Jewish-looking women walking the street."

"That's right! All the white girls are Jewish and it's normal for white guys to go out with Asian girls," Nancy said with a smile.

Daisy looked at both Tom and Nancy.

"I think we should stay a few weeks with Jake. I think we should consider moving here. Philly is nothing like this! There is a lot of cool people!" She looked back at Nancy. Knowing that two Asian girls in the car already had a connection with one another.

Nancy spotted something. "Look! Look over there!"

As Tom was waiting on a red light to turn to green, across the street was a Chinese restaurant with outside seating. It looked like two business men, with suit and tie, were talking to two Asian ladies. The one guy was using chopsticks, and the other lady was sitting right next to him.

"Look! Those guys are double dating! Both of them of them have Asian girls!"

Daisy started to laugh.

"I see them. I think both of them are Chinese."

Both of the girls stared out the same window. Nancy making the cooing noise of a bird (kind of what most kid Japanese girls like to do when they express content).

Tom looked to the left and could not see what they were looking at.

"I can't see, what's happening?" he said.

The light turned to a green. Tom kept going forward.

"There were two white guys dating Asian girls Tom," Daisy said. "Asian-Aryanism is real!"

Tom liked that thought. Maybe he should consider moving to California. Especially if California in the next few years leaves the United States. California could be the first Asian-Aryan ethno-state and an example for all nationalism to happen.

"No shit," he said in a quiet voice.

The GPS spoke back, "20-miles-until-destination,-on-right."

Tom was getting close towards Jake's house.

On the next block, there was a beach up ahead. Not only the weather was nice, it was sunny and the beach was crowded with people.

Daisy started to light up.

"Let's go to the beach!" she said is this chunky voice.

"We should totally go this week! It looks so fun!" Nancy said.

"A beach? That sounds fun. Maybe we should go, if we have the time," Tom said back like a scolding father.

"What if we have the time? Me and Daisy would have to go then by ourselves," Nancy said as a rebuttal.

"Yes! We should! Let's do that," Daisy agreed.

Both of the girls were getting giddy.

What turned from a complete stranger was now turning into close friend.

"We need to go the beach now!" Daisy said in a tiger-mom command. Her square and oval eyes along with her passive aggressive chink noise was cute.

Along with Nancy, with her baby face and bird-like goofing, was acting just as cute.

A Chinese-American girl and A Japanese-American girl getting along together and chinking and goofing like two different Asian girls bonding together would do.

Tom felt like a proud Dad. The girls were getting along fine. He didn't have to entertain Daisy all the time. Both those girls represent something he was after. He felt proud to be Daisy's boyfriend. Not only proud of that, but proud to be about of a misunderstood culture he tried to put together in his own words. California might be the answer to his happiness.

"Alright, we will go to the beach this week. It's looks fun."

Nancy pointed out something really fast.

"Look! Look! That guy is holding hands!"

"I see! I see!"

A game of punch-buggy has now turned into punch-White-Male-Asian-Female.

Both were laughing with joy.

Tom was only a few minutes away from Jake's house. He was on the same street. Simpson Street.

The road went down. The house was on a hill. Tom had to be careful were he would park. Tom texted at the last light.

"Will be there in five mins. Wait outside."

"Okay." Jake wrote.

The GPS said, "Destination,-on-right."

The house had an orange roof. Two floors sticked out with outside porches. It was slanted because of the way it was built on the hill. A typical California resident like if was based on San Francisco's Lombard Street. Tom parked the car.

A guy with a blue shirt appeared out of the house and up front of the car. Tom lowered down the front window.

"Tom, is that you?"

"Jake? It's so nice to see you!"

Both shook hands.

This was the first time they would ever meet in person. After all those Skyping and Discord sessions.

Nancy was stunned. She quickly opened the back door.

"Jake?" she said. Jake looked back at her. Jake was so surprised. It was Nancy. The girl he met on the internet and did sex stuff with. In person.

He was in a plaid blue shirt and donned a Super Mario style mustache for hipster purposes. Nancy, her fake blonde hair, and her boring green appeal.

Jake and Nancy hugged for the first time. Jake gave her kiss on the cheek.

"Nancy! How are you!?" Jake was at a loss for words. The person who know on the internet was different in person.

"Good, I'm good," she laughed. Nancy was also shy and did not know what to say.

Daisy stepped out her side of the car. Tom introduce Daisy to Jake. Jake was overwhelmingly excited. "Guys, please, come on in! I have beds upstairs for you guys stay here!"

Jake opened the door and let the guys in.

The living room was an average space. He had posters on the walls and exotic space-age furniture. Jake was into a hip style of living. He also had a huge and tall library of bizarre book. Jake went over to the library to grab the books.

"And here is *Oriental Girls* by Tom Deluge! Your own book!"

"Wow, Jake. I glad you have it. I am flattered!"

The excitement was between Jake and Tom. Jake was also excited that Nancy was here as well.

"How did you guys pick up Nancy?"

"She came for the ride."

Nancy butted in, "I found them when Tom was doing stand-out at that place you mentioned them to do..."

"Did you guys ever meet up with Rocko?"

"Yeah, Rocko was a cool guy. He's pretty funny. I promised him a podcast in the future. The whole event was super cool."

"That's awesome. I heard some guys online actually saw you at that event. Do you know of EC8OR or Himiko?"

"...No, not really..."

"Yeah, those guys saw you live! They loved it."

Daisy went back outside to go get some of her stuff to put in the house.

"Also, the guys agreed that we should stay here for a week to chill," Nancy said.

"Really? That sounds super awesome! You up for that?"

Tom scratching his own back."

"Oh yeah, totally, we can do that kind of thing," he said.

Daisy was happy with that too. She said as she was going outside.

"Yes we are!"

Jake was super thrilled.

"You guys can unpacked upstairs. There is two rooms for you guys if you need it!"

Tom went upstairs to go check the place out.

Jake approached Nancy to talk to her on private and intimate matters. For the first time, internet love became real.

Tom was in the upstairs room. It looked almost exactly like the place they stayed at last night. Again, the place had an upstairs porch to look over all the norms that walk the street. He heard Daisy coming slowly up the stairs. Tom reached out to help Daisy. "Need a hand?"

There was one single bed enough to have two people in it.

"I guess we're sleeping together tonight!" Tom said, like if it was a joke.

Daisy smiled. "I guess so."

Tom was so happy that everything was happening at the moment, he had to ask Daisy about it.

"So what do you think, nice place?"

"He seems like a nice guy. It's a nice place living in Santa Barbara. Does he own this place?"

"I don't know."

Daisy was taking of her shoes.

Tom looked back at Daisy.

"I am so glad you came Daisy. I am so grateful that we are hear together."

He was smiling like a puppy. Sometimes, Tom didn't know how to control his emotions and felt the need to express himself every moment. It was a way to fight his anxiety.

Daisy looked back at him. She smiled too.

"You're a good puppy," she said, as he patted on Tom's head. Tom had fluffy hairs. He could grew a mullet. More like skater hair.

Daisy was content at the moment. And went back downstairs to get more stuff. Tom was happy. Everything was going good. Tom laid himself on the bed to think about things for a bit.

His had nothing but optimistic thoughts.

"Wow, I can't believe that this is happening. I have an Asian girlfriend, I have another guy friend who has an Asian girlfriend, my book is getting out there, and people love my stand-up. What is next in the future? Gotta go meet Howard. This is amazing. I am finally the artist I always wanted to be since I was 14. This is amazing. I love life!" Tom thought to himself.

Everything was quiet for a bit. He felt tired from driving all day.

Daisy came up the stairs a final time to unload. She looked over at Tom.

"Were staying here, right?"

"Yep. Then we can go to the beach tomorrow!"

She smiled.

"I'm going to change into something else," she said. Daisy opened up her bad of other clothes.

Tom got up and went back downstairs to talk to Jake.

Jake was sitting in the kitchen with Nancy.

"It's so strange I met Nancy out of nowhere and like, you're so close to her!" he said.

"She was supposed to drive over to my house, but I suggested to meet up with you guys before then," Jake said.

"Mostly I took an Uber. But now I am here!" she said.

Everyone was happy.

"So, what's the plan for dinner?" Nancy asked.

"I can order some Chinese. It's on me," Jake said.

"I'm okay with that."

"Sure."

Tom had to go tell Daisy Jake was ordering Chinese.

Jake got out the menu from his cupboard.

Everyone eventually made their orders, which Jake wrote down on a piece of paper.

Now that Daisy was downstairs, Nancy had to ask Tom a question.

"How long have you two been together?"

Tom wasn't prepared to answered that question.

"We met up two months ago actually. But have been talking online forever," Tom said with pride.

"That's great. What do you guys do for fun? It's Saturday night!" she said.

"Oh, there isn't that much to do tonight. I really don't feel like going out! Honestly! Let's hang out," Daisy said as an excuse.

"Well, I have Cosmic Encounter with me. I love that game."

"Cosmic what?"

"Cosmic Encounter! It's my favorite board game, ever."

"Board game? You still play with that?"

"No, its like, a very serious board game."

"It's fun!" Daisy said.

Jake interrupted.

"Cosmic Encounter? You had those guys on your podcast, right? I heard about that game, I would love to play it."

"Yeah, it goes up to six players. We have four people!"

"That sounds awesome! I will order the Chinese now," Jake said.

"You know, you're a really interesting person Tom. You're really cool," Nancy said to him.

Tom felt flattered.

"Thank you. I mean, I don't try to be cool. Like I am some kind Johnny Bravo or some shit."

"Johnny what?"

"Nothing." Tom was laughing.

Daisy had to go to the bathroom.

Tom sat down on the couch. He still was tired today. His feet felt soar.

Nancy took a seat down next to him.

"I'm so glad I don't have to drive anymore today. I don't feel like," he said.

Tom looked up at the ceiling.

Tom, I am actually quite grateful you lent me a ride. I didn't think you would trust me at first," Nancy said.

"I don't know, you're still kind of a zombie person. You look like one."

"Really? Thanks! I try to look like a tough person. I think my hair and eyeliner gives a good impression I'm undead. I will take that as a compliment."

Tom took a deep breathe.

"But seriously, I want to thank you for driving me here. You're a really cool person. You're like, exactly like Jake. A bunch of cool white guys that like Asian girls."

Tom felt flattered. So much went on today. And then, he had to ask Nancy about something.

"Have you read my novel yet?"

"Yes, I have. I enjoyed it."

"You also know about my dreams too?"

"Yep. About how Jack wants to kill you and all that fun stuff."

Tom felt his skin crawl. Nancy was his first ever fangirl.

"I felt you were a stranger because your friend is named Suzy, and her best friend, is like, Jack, right?"

"Yep. But I have to be honest. I don't believe Suzy and Jack are the same people as in your dreams."

Tom was silent.

"What?"

"I'm pretty sure they are two of the same person in your dreams. No offense, but it's true. You did go to Villanova, didn't you? For a single semester?"

It was true. Tom did know a real life Jack and Suzy. And he was at Villanova for some time.

"Yes. Yes I do know them in person."

"Is that why you get mad? You have trauma? You should talk to me about it. I can understand."

Tom felt disgruntled. Even when the names "Jack" and "Suzy" were brought up it made him feel belittled.

"Yeah, well, if you're interested, I can tell you the whole story tonight. If you feel like it. I get into a different mood. It's too hard for me to say it, and . . . ."

"Oh, don't worry. I just want to know. This Suzy girl sounds a lot like the same Suzy you talk about in your book. You sound like you take the past way too seriously," Daisy interrupted.

The thing was, Tom did take the past very seriously.

Tom felt a little moody.

Nancy looked in right in the eyes.

"You shouldn't dwell on it. You're a really handsome guy. You look exactly like Jake!" Nancy said as she smiled.

Tom looked at her. "Thank you." He felt flattered.

"I like your hair. It's sexy."

"Haha, thank you. Everyone likes my hair!" Nancy said.

She felt her own hair.

"You can touch my hair if you like. I trust you. I wish more people were like you!"

Tom felt better about himself. Nancy was a nice person after all.

Tom caressed Nancy's hair.

"It's so fake, but it's so you."

"Thank you! I feel like a cat. Meow!"

She was acting like a little kid again. Typical of Japanese girls. Kind of sexy at the same time. Tom was a little aroused by her. Nancy was a nice person after all.

8.

Night came onto the city. A Saturday night in Santa Barbara is lively. Tom, Daisy, Jake and Nancy, were hanging out together in Jake's house. They were eating Chinese food and talking about the good times of the past. Tom's favorite was Steamed Dumplings and Jae's favorite were boneless spare ribs. There was enough food to share with the girls. After an hour of talking, everyone agreed upon playing Tom's favorite game, Cosmic Encounter. Tom had a special copy of Cosmic Encounter that suited his own algorithm of Alien powers and cards in the deck. Tom and Jake helped set up the game, while the two girls talked about familiar Asian dramas they were forced to grow up with.

"What color do you want to be Daze?"

Daisy looked at the six different colors.

"I will choose orange because Tom always chooses orange!"

"Okay, then I will have to choose red."

"Dibs on red!" Nancy yelled out.

Tom was forced to play with a different color other than his usual favorites. He chose yellow.

Jake chose purple.

"Alright, so you guys want to know how to play the game?"

"Alight."

"Sure."

Daisy already knew had to play. She remembered the first day on one date she accidentally learned Cosmic Encounter with Tom. She loved him even more for it.

"Okay . . . so, the objective of the game, is to gain five foreign colonies on five different planets. Here-here, there-there, here-there, sort of like that. Every turn, we will be attacking someone at random through the Destiny deck. You then wager one to four of your own ships on the hyperspace cone, and either of the players join your side, two players join the defenders side, both players join different sides, or things can be one-sided."

Nancy interrupted, "So wait. We can like, join each other's side and go against one another?"

"Yeah, that's the point of the game."

"This doesn't sound tradition," she said with a giggle.

Tom continued, "Now, in the card, with a hand size of 8 cards. The cards are made up Encounter cards and artifacts. Encounter cards have a number ranged from 6-40. You play these cards face down, and your opponent does the same. The winner with the highest total, including the ships counted in, is the winner. All ties go to the defender. If you win the first encounter, you may have a chance to go again. So the game is pretty much simple."

Tom dealt out eight cards to each player. Jake was taking the game seriously and was fascinated by its design. Nancy was acting goofy.

"Not only is this a traditional party game with cards, we also have a random alien power that lets us break one rule in the game."

Tom already shuffled out the alien powers and gave one to each player.

"So . . . Daisy is the loser, Nancy is the skeptic, Jake is the Trader, and I am the Macron. Each of these powers will let use break the game."

"So this is kind of like a roleplaying game?" Nancy asked.

"Exactly! Umm, for starters, let me go first and show you how a game works."

Tom often used his hands in motion to imitate the play of a how a turn works.

"First, what I do is get a ship from the warp. Because there are no ships in the warp on the first turn. So the next thing I do is I flip over the first destiny car, the player who I will be attacking."

Tom seemed like the only player interested in the game. Jake was in his own world, Nancy was joking around, and Daisy was at least trying to play like she always does. Also, Daisy was drinking a bit before they started playing. She's not drunk, but a little buzzed.

"Purple! I am attacking Jake."

"Me?"

"Yep. So I position the hyperspace gate to the planet with the least amount of ships, all the planets of have five ships, again, it doesn't matter on the first turn, and then I wager one to four ships."

"Or is it the other way around?" Daisy said with a smile.

"Whatever, this is just to show and tell."

Tom placed his little cone ships onto the paper cone thing pointing at one of Jake's planets.

"Now, Daisy or Nancy, can offer me allies."

"Wait, join sides?" Nancy asked.

"I will help Tom with four of my ships." Daisy delicately took off of four ships from four foreign colonies she owned. She placed them next to Tom's ships on the hyperspace cone.

"Wait, hold on. I don't have to join you guys, right?"

"No you don't," Tom said to Nancy.

"Join my side!" Jake said.

"Hold on. My power states that I may doubt the player if they are going to lose. So like, I am going to doubt your side Tom. I don't think you guys are going to win."

"Hah, are you sure you want to do that? Right now, it's 20 ships against four."

"Wait, 20? How are you getting that? I only see 8 ships," Jake said.

"I'm the Macron. Each one of my ships actually count as 4 ships total."

Jake was a little baffled.

"But yeah, your guys are going to lose. Give him hell Jake!"

"Umm, Okay. I think I can do this," Jake said while looking at his cards.

Tom explained the rules further.

"We are going to take down a number card, put it face down like this, and simultaneously reveal the said card."

Tom put down a card as an example.

"Okay, umm, so, I think I got it."

Jake put down his face down card.

Both cards were down.

"Now let's reveal," Tom said.

Tom had had a six card, and Jake had a big 40 card.

44 against 26. Jake's side had won.

"Awesome! What do I win?"

Nancy butted in, "Ha! You guys did lose! So you lose more ships than usual! You guys suck!"

"Alright, I guess Jake won, and the Skeptic power comes in."

Daisy, a little buzzed, interrupted.

"Hold on! Guys, I'm the loser. Do you know what that does? Whenever your side loses, they win, and whenever your side wins, they lose. So technically, we lost. We actually won!"

"Wait, what?" Nancy looked at Daisy's power.

"Huh?" Jake siad in confusion.

Everyone was now in conflict with the rules.

"I don't think that's exactly how the loser works," Tom said.

"Yes, it fucking does! Take a look!" Nancy said. "Motherfucker! Fuck you, Daisy!"

Daisy was laughing. Jake too.

Tom didn't want to be the jerk imposing rules.

"So yeah, Daisy did win. And we won. All of Jake's ship goes to the warp and me, and Daisy gets one foreign colony on Jake's planet's. Daisy and I are four foreign colonies away from winning the game."

"Wait, so you guys can have shared wins in this game?" Nancy said.

"Yeah, sure. So long as everyone agrees upon the climatic encounter and stuff like that."

"Fucking sick," Nancy said.

And so twenty minutes into the game they were already having fun. The flow became more frequent and Jake and Nancy was starting to understand the game. They might have been goofing up the rules, but who cares? The point was that they were having fun.

Jake was in the lead with three foreign colonies, followed by Nancy with two.

Nancy was getting restless. She took out a roll of marijuana from her pocket. Along with a lighter.

"I need a smoke, it feels so much better."

Nancy smoked and puffed on her ganja.

"Pass me over some too, boo," Jake said. Nancy passed over the weed too Jake. Jake puffed on it. "This is okay," he said. "Do you want some Tom?"

"Weed? I don't know. I never tried it before."

"What? You never had it? You should. Ever smoke?"

"Umm, no not really, I never had a chance."

Nancy was getting excited.

"It sounds like someone is a virgin. You should totally break that tonight!"

Peer pressure was forming around Tom.

"Daisy, do you want a smoke?"

"I don't know. I mean, it smells kind of disgusting and like, nah I'll pass."

Daisy took another shot of her cold beer. She was cool.

"But dude, totally try it. It's not bad at all. It's like coke, like, sugar soda," Nancy persuaded to Tom.

Jake was flying the cigar in his face while the smoke followed it.

Tom grabbed pretend to smoke it.

"What do I do? Put my lips on it and blow?" Tom then trying to imitate a smoker's lips. He really didn't know how to smoke at all.

"Nah, just like, blow on it till it burns," Jake said.

Tom pushes his lips on the weeds. He smoked on it a bit, a reacted in a strange way.

"Ah, eww. It's kind of . . . ."

"Gross?" Nancy was laughing. "Try it again."

Tom tried to blow on it again. Daisy was laughing. Daisy herself was a weed advocate and knew good weed from bad. Tom was smoking bad weed.

Tom this time got a good blow from it. Smoke coming from it. He had to pass it to Nancy.

He made some grumble noises. He didn't know how to define the taste.

"No, like you moron!" Nancy smoked on the blunt like some kind of cartoon character. She was overdramatizing and making fun of how Tom smoked it. She blew out smoke like a dragon that blows fire. "Ah, it's good now. Shit. Whose turn it is?"

"Oh, wait, it's mine," Daisy said.

She flipped over the next destiny card.

Everyone still was having fun. Tom was feeling less anxious. He felt like he was on puffy white clouds. Everyone was at peace, playing his favorite game and acting all too real.

The game would really strange at times. On Tom's turn, Jake asked a question about stripped planets. Tom tried to explain,

"If you have, no more colonies on each of those planets, you lose your alien power. You have to draw your own destiny color in order to get ships back on your planet. Unless you were like, that bull dude aliens, you couldn't move from that planet."

"Bull dude? There is that in the game? Did you guys ever see my bull ring?" Nancy was a bit high.

90

"Look at this!" She pulled down her green tank top to reveal her left tit. A round piercing was in it. "See this?" She was flashing at everyone.

"Whoa, that's kind of cool. Who did that?" Jake said.

"A friend did it. Tom touch it!"

Daisy was laughing it.

Tom felt a little aroused.

Nancy was shaking her left tit like it was fat on her stomach.

Jake touched her nipple. "It feels so soft." Tom went in a touch her nipple with his finger. To sound funny, he said, "Boink!"

Nancy was giggling. "I know right? My tit is still soft even with the bull ring in it. Do you think it's fucking cool guys?

"Yes, it's super cute," Tom said.

Daisy was laughing.

"Daisy, let me see your titties! Whose titties are bigger?"

"Mine? Really? Haha, should I?"

"Go ahead," Tom said very awkwardly.

Daisy took off her pajama top to reveal her naked, flat chest. In the size contest, Nancy's tits were a little bit bigger. Daisy's tits were petite and cute. Healthy looking as well.

"Were naked!" Daisy said.

"Yes we are!" Nancy said like a little kid. She was into these kind of kiddie little things. Being naked felt like they were little kids talking about bathroom jokes.

Daisy had her shirt off and Nancy awkwardly exposing her left tit. "Alright Tom, what card are you going to play?"

Tom lost his reason to play. His lust was getting to him. Both Nancy and Daisy looked sexy. He felt like he should undress too.

"Okay, here I go," Tom said as he continued the game. Daisy laughed as she put her shirt back on.

"Tom likes licking my titties a lot!" Daisy said in a drunken mood.

"I bet he does!" Nancy laughed.

She made this French kissing licking motion while teasing Tom. Jake was laughing as well. Tom felt he was under the control of two vixens.

The game continued back and forth with raunchy jokes like this. Everyone enjoyed playing Cosmic Encounter and everyone got closer to one another. Eventually, Daisy and Nancy won the game by a joint victory. Tom lost concentration after the titty flashing and the weed in his system.

It was already pass midnight. Tom didn't feel like cleaning up the game, as he felt he could do not tomorrow. This would be the first night of many. Everything felt so good. Daisy passed out on the sofa. "I'm going to sleep guys. ...Nancy, I will be in my room if you want to come sleep. Otherwise, I got a bed right there."

"Thanks Jake, but I'm pretty hammered. I think I will crash there."

"Awesome," Jake said like it was a day dream.

Tom felt a bit off. Was this the side effect of the weed he smoked? He felt really happy, but tired at the same time. He was in the bathroom washing his hands. Daisy was passed out on the sofa and could not get up to her room. Tom walked upstairs and changed into his pajamas. He laid on the bed, looking up at the ceiling. He turned off the lights.

And then Nancy came into the room. She sat on his side the bed.

"What? Are you going to sleep right now? I am fucking out of it right now."

"Yeah well, I am pretty tired at the moment, so . . . ."

"Wait, I didn't get to see you naked yet. Pull down your pants."

Tom was confused.

"What?"

"I said pull down your pants. I didn't get to see that cock of yours. I want to see what you're really like."

"Wait, why?"

"You saw my titties, I want to see it."

Nancy sat so close to him and tom was too lazy to sit up out of bed.

Jokingly, he said, "Yeah, here it is," as he quickly pulled down his pajama shorts and back up again.

"Holy shit! Let me see it again!"

Tom felt horny and confused.

He pulled down his pants. He had a full bush of pubic hairs. Unapologetic to shave it.

Nancy was laughing. "Not bad! I like it! Very manly!"

"Yeah, that's my dick, happy now?"

Nancy had something else in mind. The door was closed. The room was dark. The only light in the room came from the city lights outside.

'Are you horny? I will jerk you off," she said in a whisper.

Tom was confused. He was horny . . . but, jerking him off?

"Wait, why?"

"I want to see you shoot. I want to see how much you can shoot out. You're a cool guy."

Already within 24 hours this girl wanted to jerk off Tom.

Daisy was downstairs. Tom could not resist the urge. He was aloof and high.

"Sure, uhh . . . play with it and sees what happens."

Tom was in a date rape situation. Nancy was raping Tom.

"Ok!" Nancy then was playing with Tom's dick like how a cat throws a mouse. Then she started jerking it off and tried to get blood pumping through Tom's penis.

"Do you like when I do this?" she said in a quiet tone.

"Yeah," Tom said with a smile.

He lost control of his own self. A pretty Japanese girl was jerking of Tom's dick. He did nothing but stare in silence at the beauty of Nancy.

His dick was hard and stiff. She was jerking his big cock like she'd done this many times before.

"It's a really nice cock, Tom. I'm glad you're letting me touch it," she said.

Tom was blushing and quite happy. He didn't know anything anymore.

Within five minutes, he shot sperm up in the air. And the rest flooded all over Nancy's jerking hand.

She was laughing.

And Tom was then blacking out.

9.

Tom was in a deep sleep. What happen before was a daydream. He fell quickly to sleep after Nancy kissed him on the head. His pants down, and his blanket over his body. Tucked in like a little kid.

He was in a different place now. His dreams were like a different reality.

Tom woke chained to the ground. He was on his knees. Lifting his arms, he could not break free from the chain and shackle tied to him. He was in a dark room of unknown origin. A void, black room.

Tom was breathing heavy.

Across the room sat a man on a throne. He had no head, but a fancy outfit made for a prince.

"Listen to me, Thomas. Listen to me."

The loud voice came echoing through him. Tom was staring at the dark spirit known as Jack. Behind his throne, showed an endless horizon of a red ocean. Something only in a dream that could happen.

Jack was a headless prince. A shapeshifter of many sorts. He was always a different creature in Tom's sleep.

Possibly, Tom was going through a chemical imbalance and his dream was a mixture of everything happening. From meeting Nancy and Jake for the first time, smoking weed for the first time, that hand job, way too much stuff in a single day. But he was not aware of this in his sleep.

A loud voice raced through Tom's head. Anxiety. What he hated the most. The feeling of not belonging. The urge to try and do good. Failure.

A picture of a strong white man and his Korean wife gazed upon him. He was 26, she 24. Married. Tom was 25. He was not like that. He was a loser.

Picture of couple's raced through his head. He was a camera that saw every little thing in his college years. The white guys, their Asian girls, the video-game club. Hopelessness.

...Suzy. That thing Nancy knows. They she tormented Tom every day. Calling him "tommy" to sound like he was still in elementary school.

Tom was an average guy with an average built. How could he have ever wooed over an Asian girl like Daisy? Is he really all that handsome? Or is really a weakling that projects his traumas onto the world?

Tom was now sitting on the train with no arms. Jack looking straight at him. Jack, with his brown hairs and shady beard, the face that would haunt Tom. Just starring at him. And then he smiled.

...What does Nancy know about a Jack and Suzy? Where does she belong in this?

Tom was back chained to the floor. Many pictures raced through his head. All of this didn't make any sense. He felt like screaming. He was screaming at nothing.

Jack said something strange to Tom.

"She's mine. You can't have her. I know you want her. But she's mine. You can't have her. I know you want her. But she's mine. You can't have her. I know you want..."

Over and over again, this chant would ring through Tom's ears.

...He remembers the day that girl gave him his first blowjob in bed. He was 18 at the time. And that girl told him she loved him. And he would go after her... until the age of 23, she told him he was cheating on him. Terrible.

And it was only last year Tom would be texting her again before he suddenly met Daisy.

Jack was teasing Tom with all these traumas. The traumas that made Tom feel like a loser. That thoughts that made him cry in bed every night.

...Suddenly, Tom woke up. He was alone in his room. A dark room. The room was empty. Half naked in his bed. Daisy was still downstairs sleeping on the sofa.

What was exciting before, turned into nightmares?

Tom wanted to cry alone. He thought about the first girl he ever loved... Mary. Then Lisa. And now Stacy. Those girls would never get away from him. He could not treat as all universal. All these girls were Asian. The pain that he made the wrong choice in life. Trying to be himself and these girls hated him for it. If he was someone else, like a muscular jock or an independent norm, maybe he would be able to woo Mary over. Even Lisa. ...Even Stacy.

Tom cried alone in his bed. He cried feeling a deep passion of loneliness. He remembered the times he cried talking to his mom and his brother about girls he could not woo over. They would never understand. They just gave him comfort.

On his 21st birthday, Mary failed to come over to his house. It rained that day. And only his autistic friend George came over to greet him. He couldn't have his way. His life was nihilistic living out in bumfuck retired suburbia.

Deep shit.

Was the first 25 years of his life wasted? Was he actually an autistic loner and he didn't know it? Could of it been spent living in California, having a young wife, and accomplishing his wild his dreams has an avant-garde artist?

Why was he starting so late? Is he still overcoming his trauma he had from his verbally abusive father and overprotective and naive mother? Is it because he is an only child? Is he an innate coward and unnaturally afraid of rejection?

All those things are consider. That is what Jack teased him about every day of Tom's life.

He was crying. Nothing made sense anymore.

...But then after that long hour of crying. His tears dried up.

...He had Daisy. He had a new friend called Jake. Nancy gave him a hand job. That's some kind of adventure. And now he is in California. Only the best are allowed in the state.

The dark room was turning a blue. Tom would usually get up and walk around for a bit, until he thought of happy things. Not right now. He had to calm himself down until the thoughts went away.

...Daisy. Daisy his love. He hopes Daisy does not find out a complete stranger gave him a hand job. No.

...Jack is not real. Jack is figment of Tom's imagination. ...Based upon a kid he knows in real life.

Justin.

His crying began again. Closing his eyes, thinking how much he wants to get revenge on this kid named Justin. Every jerk he has every met in his life had the name of Justin. There was Justin in the 8th grade with muscles that used the gym. There was a Justin into metalcore that bully Tom in high school. And there was Justin that was the president of the board game club that hot Asian girlfriend...

It was too much for him to handle. His face. Over and over again. Like a dark puppet that haunted him. The puppet that would haunt his senior year of college. The creature that became Jack.

...and then, he was back to sleep.

Like that. All his anger. All his rage. Was quickly forgotten.

This next dream was different.

Tom was at the airport. An airport filled with green plants and trees. A jungle was inside this complex. And there was Lisa. The girl he met on a college dating website. Her avatar picture was nice, so he approached her. Only 22 at the time, when everything was getting rocky with Mary. Lisa had a nice face and kind personality. They finally met once in real life. Only for Tom to hear that she was not interested in hanging out. He only got a kiss on the cheek.

...But in this this dream, he was cumming on her face. Like a water fountain. Her cute, chunky and pushy Chinese face, being ejaculated on by his dick. The shots of sperm coming out of him, like a water gun. All over her face. She was opening her mouth and swallowing the sperm. He kept ejaculating on her. Tom felt the sensation in his dream.

Lisa would run with her naked body. Tom would chase after her with his long cock he could trip over with his feet. He kept shooting sperm at her like a laser gun. Every shot hitting her body. Chasing her around in this jungle airplane land. Everything felt so good.

...And then everything was black again. Everything felt peaceful. No more Jack. An innocent picture of Lisa dominated his mind.

And then he was sitting alone in a plane. A plane that would take him somewhere. Through the orange clouds he was going.

...Orange was his favorite color.

A soft a nice dream that was normal.

...Tom woke up.

The sun was up.

Everything was but a dream. A scary one. Dried tears on his pillow. His sheets mixed up into a single ball laying on his legs. Crazy. What is it real?

Nancy walked in. She didn't realize Tom just woke up.

Tom had to say something.

"Hey!" he said, in his tired voice.

Nancy spied over. She was getting something out of the bathroom. "Hey!" she said back.

"Where's Daisy?"

"She's on the sofa. I think she's okay. Are you okay?"

She had a smile on her face. Like she knew what was up.

"Please, don't tell Daisy anything," Tom said in a grouchy voice.

Nancy came over to sit on his side on the bed.

"I won't. I was having too much fun last night. ...I thought you're a cool guy."

Tom didn't realize Nancy was a whore.

"Please, please don't tell her, ok?"

"I won't. You have my trust!"

Nancy was playing on her mp3 player. Bluetooth to her speaker in the same room. She was going to play a song.

"Bad girl! Bad girl!" followed by a loud synthesizer.

Tom curled his head in bed.

"Do you like Eurobeat? I love Eurobeat. I loved it growing up," she said.

"Uh-ah," Tom said.

The wacky and bouncy synth lead came in. Tom was a Eurobeat aficionado too.

The singer was Elena Gobbi. Known for her acts as Virginelle and Lolita.

And that chorus came in. Nancy was singing as she was putting away clothes.

"That's why they call me BAD GIRL! I'm your lover teacher! Bad is Bad and you want me honey!"

It was a really good song. One of Gobbi's best.

A bad girl indeed. She sang it like she took pride in the term.

..She was kind of cute. The way she moved her butt. The strutting she did, the singing. Very baby like.

But she was not that innocent type. A type of beautiful flower with thorns around her.

Tom had to get up.

He moved out of bed, pulled up his pants, and headed to the bathroom.

...That wacky synth line was very catchy.

Tom was brushing his teeth, looking at himself in the mirror.

"Bad is bad! ...want me honey!"

Still she was singing in the other room.

Tom had to approach her.

"Nancy? I just wanted to say... you are really cool person."

Nancy looked back at him.

"Also, please don't tell Jake any of that happen last night!"

"Ok."

He should forget what happened last night. Especially with that dream he had too.

Tom was pulling down his pants to get on his underwear and day shorts. Orange shorts.

"You have a nice cock Tom! Very masculine!" She said.

What a tease! And he thought she would drop it now.

He better check on Daisy.

Downstairs, Daisy was having morning tea. She had a hangover.

"Ugghhhh..." is the only thing that came out of her.

Tom approached Daisy.

"Hey babe! You ok?"

"Yeah. Just, not gonna drink for the next week."

"Yeah, you don't usually drink, do you?"

"It was a special occasion. It was worth."

Tom thought about how unreal everything was last night.

Daisy was laughing.

"So you like my tits a lot, do you?"

"Huh?"

"Last night. That tit contest, I had the best tits, right?"

"Absolutely. You had the best tits!"

Things with Daisy were good. She was having fun too last night too.

"Hey, where's Jake?"

"Oh yeah, he told me he had to go get... supplies at a store. He will be back later. He said you should meet up with Howard."

Tom checked out his phone. He had several text from Jake about telling to meet up with Howard today. Another text he got from Howard too.

"Want to meet at 5th street today at 1PM?"

That's what he has to do today.

"Do you want to come along with me?"

"You know... I think I'm going to go on the beach with Nancy. She is such a cool person."

Oh shit. Hope Nancy doesn't tell what happens last night. That's a little... well, he can trust her.

"Alright, sounds cool."

"I'm excited. Nancy is really cool. I finally found a nice girlfriend to hang out with. She's such a good person. I feel like she's some kind of sister."

Already? It's only been 24 hours and this bond is happening. It's happening to Daisy too.

"That's great!"

Tom looked at the clock. It was 12 noon. He should get ready and go see Howard.

Nancy came bouncing down the stairs in a blue bra and pants.

"How I look for the beach?"

"Super cute! I like it!" Daisy said.

Tom noticed a tattoo on her left arm.

"Wait, what's that?"

"This? Oh, it's X-Japan. Favorite band ever!"

...so she's that kind of person.

Tom headed upstairs to get change in a better shirt. First time meeting Howard as well. The girls were getting ready to go out too. Daisy had to find a suit to wear to the beach.

...It sure was a sunny day out today. A super sunny day. A nice day. It's felt paradise. Too much paradise.

10.

Tom took the car down to Maple Street to meet up with Howard. Nancy and Daisy were in walking distance of the beach. Jake was out for appliances, or something.

For the first time, Tom would meet up with Howard Fesler, the host of The Hoedown Truth. Tom is a co-host for the show. He has been doing for a year and a half now. Howard told him to come down to Santa Barbara to meet him. Along with Jake, who promised to publish Tom's next book. It was Howard that opened doors for Tom to become a well know internet celebrity and touring comedian. And most importantly, an avant-garde novelist. His dreams were coming true. Thanks to Howard.

Tom wanted to make a good impression on Howard. Jake is a pretty laid back kind of guy. Tom expected the same from Howard. Howard would be chill.

That's what he thought.

Tom parked outside a nearby Park. He would meet with Howard some feet away. Tom texted Howard with an update.

"I'm here. Where are you?"

"At Johnny's Calms."

Tom saw Johnny's Calms up ahead.

Walking towards it, he saw two men. One with brown hair in a nice dress and the other guy looking like a beatnik. The man waved his arm. Tom waved his. He came running up towards them.

"Fesler? Hey! Howard! How are you?"

For the first time, Tom got to meet his boss and hero in person.

"Hi Inkdrinker!" Howard greeted Tom.

Inkdrinker was Tom's fake name he used on the internet.

They were so happy to meet each other in person.

"Hey, I would like you to meet Turtle!"

Turtle was an internet poet and inventor of Alt-twee. An alternative viewpoint from traditional norms of Twee. His book "Dada Communism" was widely circulated around the Alt-twee circle.

Turtle dressed nice like a real life beatnik. His favorite aesthetically pleasing film was Logan's Run, and wished everything in reality was like it.

"Where did you want to go eat at?" Howard said.

"I don't know. What did you guys have in mine?"

"What about Thai food? I know that's Inkdrinker's favorite food!"

A funny joke.

"Wait, let me take a picture with you guys."

Howard had a special camera and was interested in photography. He took photos where ever he went. He took a group photo of Inkdrinker, Turtle, and Howard. He took another photo of Inkdrinker and Turtle. And then took another photos of Johnny's Calm.

And then they were off to the Thai restaurant.

Walking down Maple Street, Tom recollected his journey with him and Daisy and how they got to Jake's house. He talked about the disgusting venue in Arizona and the crazy people he met. Howard was taking a picture of every building he passed by.

"So no one is actually hostile towards Asian-Aryanism?" Turtle asked.

"Nope. Everyone loves it. It's going good. I hope to get the next book out on Jake's publishing house."

"Do you think he will publish my book?" Howard asked.

"I think he would love that. He's looking for other works too."

"I want as many people to read it as possible," Howard said.

A blonde woman past by them as they were walking. Howard looked back.

"Inkdrinker, did you see that?"

"See what?"

"That woman."

"That woman?"

"Yeah, her. She's uhh... totally I.A."

I.A. was a spinoff of Tom's Asian-Aryanism. Israeli-Aryanism. Howard had something for the blonde, Jewish looking women.

"Oh Howard. Is your book going to manifest that idea?"

"Yeah why not. You're having a crazy amount of success. I should do it too."

Howard was influence by everyone he had on his podcast.

"Where's Alex? Where you going to meet up with him?"

"No. I don't know. I never met the guy," Tom said.

Howard wanted everything perfect. His OCD was kicking in.

"Hey, we're here at the place, let's go in," Turtle said.

They sat down together in a quiet room. They could talk about anything.

Tom didn't want to buy something crazy, so he went with the usual General Tso's chicken. Howard was looking to get something expensive.

"So Inkdrinker, what drew you in into the whole Asian chick thing?" Turtle asked.

"Well, it was something I witnessed all throughout my high school and undergrad years at college. When I got back home, I felt like I could not shake off the trauma I experienced at such a young age. I don't think I should move on and forget about my experiences. I can really only go forward if I express my trauma now," Tom said.

"The only really nice things I have to say about Asians is that they make nice foods and give really good back massages. I am not talking about the 'happy ending' kind, I am talking about in general."

"I can understand. I feel that there are too many young people hanging out with Asian girls and keeping it a secret. I don't know why they go out about, but it's there."

Howard interrupted.

"Or the fact that most rich people in California all have blonde Jewish women," he said as a joke.

"But this is serious Howard. The numbers of White-male/Asian-female is overwhelming. It's the only thing that this multicultural paradigm has given us. It's this phenomena no one wants to talk about. Blonde Jewish women is totally a joke."

Howard was a practical prankster. Tom was close enough to him to understand he was joking.

The waiter came and everyone gave in an order for food.

The talking began again.

"I wish the world was like, more like mod girls of the 1960's," Turtle said.

"In no way am I trying to push that everyone should get an Asian girlfriend. What I am saying is that it is happening and no one is talking about it. I think the whole men-going-their-own-way would benefit if they found out about Asian women," Tom said.

"I will be honest with you. The only Asian girls I knew were like in high school. There were like three of them and they all sat together. And their favorite bands were like, Panic! at the Disco, Simple Plan, Good Charlotte, My Chemical Romance, HIM. Really cheesy stuff that was so popular in the early 2000s. They only liked those bands because I think they just wanted to fit in or find themselves a cute, white boyfriend really."

"I think that's true too. But those bands totally sound like mega douches bags. Good girls like Yellow Music Orchestra, Placebo, Sandii and the Sunsets, Haley Kiyoko. Anything from vintage, street or twee."

"What about vaporwave?" Howard asked.

Tom thought about it.

"Sure, why not. But I think Asian-Aryanism has its own music aesthetic and culture. It's there totally. No one is classifying it."

The appetizers came over. Pizza rolls. Howard had to take a picture of the pizza rolls. Then he passed the camera over to Turtle.

"Turtle, can you take a picture of me while I am eating this?"

Howard made a funny face while he took a bit into the roll.

"Ok... Hold on."

A flash from the camera. Howard had to take a picture of every moving thing.

Tom smiled.

"Should we do the next podcast meeting up and spying on the women in Santa Barbara?" he said.

"Oh wait! Maybe we should do a quick movie while we are outside and call it 'the official first meeting of the Alt-twee movement'"

"Let's do that later!" Turtle said.

All were enjoying the food.

"Pizza rolls? What do you make of it?" Tom said.

"Eurasian White/Asian, Asian-Aryan food," Howard laughed.

"That's strange to think about, an Italian-Chinese mixed person. Would that be like Super Mario?" Turtle said.

"Interesting, I'm not sure what to make of that," Tom said in confusion.

He took a bite out of a pizza roll.

"So what did you major in?" turtle asked to Tom.

"I majored in English and communications. A double major. It was a way to make sense of an already useless degree. Although I think to myself as an Asian Studies major with an interested in the arts. That would best describe me."

"Where did you graduate from?"

Tom looked nervous.

"Oh, some girl's school that opened up for guys. I really hated the place after two years. Tons of bitchy people there. I felt alone. The professors hated me too. I don't know why they hated me there. I tried my best to be good. I don't like to talk about it.

"Most kids today don't even make it out of college today with the whole social justice warrior and anti-white take over that's happening now."

"Thanks. But... I feel I could have had a better experience. ...So I want to get into grad school actually. I think I can do Creative Writing, or some two year degree. I can do it."

"Totally. Go for it if you have the money! I'm going back to community college and getting an associate's in the fine arts. Community college is much more laid back and awesome. Nobody goes to college to learn about anything anymore. It's a lost tradition. They steal your money and assume you know things that are you own parents teach you."

"I can understand that. I feel that way about the schools I went to. And I jumped from four different colleges. Still, I'm not sure if I learned anything proper."

"...D you plan on using your degree to do something with work?"

"I plan on writing books and selling them. Art is my capital. I don't want to teach. That is a super cucked and default position. I don't want to talk to blacks or strangers. They don't need my advice. I want to work for myself. I will however consider a job from a corporation in the future. I will try it out. Not sure if I will like it."

"It's super competitive and you have to dress and shave every other day. Though I heard you can get benefits from it."

"Yeah you're right about that part."

Tom finished his roll.

"So why did you go for English then?" Turtle asked.

"...because I didn't know how to write a paper and I wanted to improve my writing skills. That's all. I didn't sign up for European white man history or any French critical theory philosophy. I flirted with white nationalism and now I am returning what I really wanted to do... Asian Studies."

"But why not continue to learn Asian Studies and get a degree in that?"

"Because I would have had to take three extra years of Japanese when in reality, I was in it to get the degree and walk out. I will focus on learning Japanese in the future. Edward Seidensticker said the same thing about his education with English. Completely useless until he devoted himself to a new hobby. ...I was in English because all my credits matched that path. I could take anything I wanted to... and I was told that by my parents... but there is no degree or work for doing something you love. I could try and go for business. I hate math. I could have tried phycology or meds... don't like science either. But would have considered for the hot Asian girls now. I feel like I am a free spirit and English was the only way to go. At the same time, however, I disagree with the practice of English and I hate the whole school of linguistics. IT's the very thing that is going against our red pill generation."

"I see," turtle was listening. "Don't bother with that shit. They are prudes to begin with. They don't understand you heart or what you are doing."

"I feel like they are flawed and I was abused and exploited be an institution that made me feel like a little baby. ...But you're right. I don't have to submit to them any longer. I can do my own things as an adult finally. As an adult, I want to get a Masters in Fine Arts. I think I can do it. I have the money in the trust fund. I can do it for two years. I don't care what I do with it. I need the degree to show I have class. I need to be an elitist and change people's minds!"

"Go for it dude! That's all I can say."

Tom left his thoughts at that. Anxiety ruled his day to day living.

"Are you going to write a new book?" Howard asked.

"I think so. I don't know what it will be about."

"Why don't you talk about Elliot Rodger and his manifesto?"

"No way. That's s way too edgy."

"Or what about writing a manifesto of the Asian-Aryan ideology."

"No. Not going to do that either. I don't know what more I can say on that."

Howard believed in Tom. Tom could write about anything.

"Will you help edit my book with it's out?"

"I will Howard. It's going to be good when you get it out. Maybe Jake can get it out."

"He can?"

"Sure. If he wants to publish my own book, he can do yours too."

Already plans for the future looked good.

After several minutes of talking about the usual, the main entree was ready.

The crew was finally together long at last.

11.

After enjoying a feast together, the gang was back on Maple. So much of Tom's life was covered in two hours.

"...Seriously, I would love to have a sitcom about the Asian-Aryan life. It could be like a really cheesy 90's rival show. It would be something like *100 Deeds for Eddie McDowd* or like that cartoon *The Undergrads*. It's like, the guy has an Asian girlfriend, and gets into all this calamity with life and underground culture. And the show could have a really cheesy pop-punk intro, like by Reggie and The Full Effect or Reel Big Fish. Totally non-Asian-Aryan bands, but the point is, it's about the 90's ethics and getting the message across about hip SWPL culture. I should make this into my next comedy skit," Tom thought.

"Wait, I remember that cheesy cartoon The Undergrads. Wasn't the girl on that show Asian too? That's already perfect," turtle said.

"Yep, I think so."

"Oh man. Inkdrinker, you're really obsessed with Asian girls," Howard said.

"...It's the point where my trauma is becoming a self-sustaining career. I am always looking out for how I can express myself and how I can get cash at the same time."

Tom took pride in what he was doing. This wasn't a joke. His life was significant.

"If you guys learned any instruments, we should start a pop-punk band right now. My lyrics would be only about why I hate this one Asian girl I met in college. It would be totally funny as shit and awesome!"

"I don't know Inkdrinker, I'm not into that kind of music. I am already doing something on my Bontempi keyboard. The minimal bachelor pad music would get in your way," Turtle said jokingly.

"Come to think of it, how music for Israeli-Aryanism go?" Howard asked.

"Good question. Don't you like vaporwave Howard?"

"..That can work. Like disco stuff. Like Fashwave or some kind of Italo-Disco. That sounds good."

The guys were having a fun time.

They walked straight passed a homeless vagabond begging for money. He had on a "Dystopia" shirt.

"Spare change sir! Spare change! Need it!"

Tom looked at the so-called homeless man. He passed him a business card with his website on it.

Tom whispered to Turtle and Howard. "That guy is a total faker. See his shirt? Some hardcore band no one gives a shit about. Totally SWPL. I think white people love to

LARP as some oppressed person against the system, like they are looking for attention."

"What makes you think that?"

"See his dreads? White people love getting dreads. The West Coast would be so much better without all these White hippies and Roleplay anarchist. They should all do something more productive!"

Tom's phone was beeping. He received a text message. Checking his phone, it was a cute selfie of Daisy and Nancy on the beach together.

"Guys! Have you seen my girl? I'm not kidding! This is her. She is on the beach with another hot Asian girl we met. This is her."

Tom showed his phone to Turtle and Howard.

Howard was laughing.

"She is cute," Turtle said.

"It's amazing! I know. I'm going to marry her. This is it. I waited for this day for so long. I don't when I am going to propose. I am planning on putting down money for a house and finding constant work schedule somewhere."

"This is the place to do it Inkdrinker. Move to Santa Barbara. We can hang out all the time"

"Please Howard! You got to help find me a place to stay here! I am staying at Jake's house for a week, and I need direction."

"Dude, it's quite affordable to live outside the city. Only 20 minutes away. I would consider that," Turtle said.

"Wow. ...You guys gotta meet Jake. He's a super cool person."

"The guy you met on Discord?"

"Yeah. He's been living here too. Such a coincidence! Maybe he would offer me space and we can live together."

"It sounds like you guys are becoming one big family!" Howard said.

"I know right?"

Tom sound so eager for his future plans.

He texted back to Daisy.

"Awesome! With the guys!"

Attached was a group picture he took of him, Howard and Turtle.

What an awesome day it was.

Up ahead, a shady looking girl was talking to people. She looked right at Tom. She was a dark skin Asian with fishnets and books. It likely was a prostitute.

"Hey there! What's your name?" she said to Tom.

The guys looked back at him.

"Tom, who are you?"

"I'm Cleo, where are you headed stud muffin?"

...It was one of those girls.

Turtle said to her, "Sorry lady, we are not interested in your business."

"Oh really? Why not?"

Tom could tell she was some kind of Asian. She looked Vietnamese or Indonesian.

"Have you ever heard of Asian-Aryanism?" Tom said back to her.

He was trying to impress his friends.

"No, what's that?"

"It's when white guys hook up with Asian girls and Asian guys hook up with White girls and group together for their own interest. You might be an Asian-Aryan princess."

Howard was laughing.

"That sounds wonderful? Am I your princess?"

"So as long you support love between the two races and have a white boyfriend."

Tom reached for his card to give to her.

You should check out some on my stuff I do." Tom said as he head along.

She looked at the card.

"Wow! Thanks! I will call you, Sweetie!"

Turtle and Howard were laughing as they were walking away from her.

"Inkdrinker. That was crazy. You gave that Asian hooker your contacts."

"Yep. One small step for Asian-Aryanism. Watch her turn all her customers into them too. She's a walking soldier.""

"That was so mad," turtle said.

Both the guys laughing at Tom's amazing skills as an Asian-Aryan advocate.

Tom got another text. This text was from Jake.

"Yo! You home? Want to do something?"

This could be the perfect opportunity for him to meet the guys.

Tom texted back, "Howard and Turtle are with me. Want to meet them?"

They were back on Johnny's Calms.

"Inkdrinker, you are here for a full week right?"

"Yes I am."

"I have to go back home and get ready for evening classes. We should hang later tonight."

"Jake's house! Do you have his address? I will send it."

"Okay, that sounds good. 8PM?"

"Totally."

"I'm coming along the ride too," Turtle said. "We should hang tonight!"

Thirty minutes later, after shooting the breeze about life and fun stuff, Howard and max were off together and promise to meet Tom at Jake's house around 8. Howard had to take one picture of the group one last time.

"Turtle, I think we need battery for my camera. Let's head to Walgreen's for it."

"Alight, see you then Inkdrinker!"

Tom waved goodbye to his friends. He headed back to his car.

Totally chilled time it was.

Tom was driving back to Jake's house.

Santa Barbara was such a nice city. Nice weather, cute Asian and White couples, Asian hookers in the street, a little SWPL culture, everything seemed so right about the place.

Tom was looking at the beach as he was driving.

"I wonder what Daisy and Nancy are doing right now?"

He imagined them both skimming water at one another in their sexy bathing suits. Like some kind of playful high school anime drama by the beach. Both of them were cuties. Tom feels grateful he gets to come home to both of them.

Tom tuned in on the radio. One station had on classical New Jack Swing. He turned the dial to a news station. A new reported with a loud voice was talking about a terrorist attack on New York by an unknown force. It sounded very interesting, but Tom could care less. He's not in New York at the moment.

Tom parked the car outside Jake's house. It didn't feel like no one was home. Tom opened the front door with the keys and stepped inside.

He got off his shoes and laid on the couch. Tom felt like watching cartoons. He turned on the TV. On the TV instead was a giant pentagram. A big red pentagram. Tom flicked onto the next channel, still a pentagram. Did this have something to do with what the news reporter was saying on the radio?

Suddenly, a man walked into the room behind Tom. The man had no head and wore a nicely dressed purple robe.

"Thomas. Listen to me. This is becoming a reality!" he said in a chilling voice.

Tom turned head. It was him. The man without a head. Jack. His evil spirit that haunted him in his dreams.

Tom scared shitless, he ran to the door. The door was locked. Jack used his satanic powers to stun Tom from running.

"Come with me. I have to talk to you," the phantom said.

Opened a portal in the middle of the room. The portal vacuumed Tom in it. Tom was screaming.

His nightmare was a true monster he could not control.

Down the vortex, Tom fell on the wooden raft in a sea of red water. Jack slowly gravitated next to him.

"What the fuck do you want!?" Tom was screaming.

"Tom, it is I, Jack. And I finally have reached the outer world in order to comfort your desires."

Tom tried to jump in the ocean to run away, but Jack's power was strong enough that he could not.

"Thomas, I have been watching you in your sleep every night. And I have successfully lead you to this final destination here at Santa Barbara."

Tom's kin was crawling. Jack's voice was one reverb after another.

"You're going to release me out of this world, Tom. You have given birth to new devil child there will destroy this Earth to create a new one."

"What the fuck is that?" Tom yelled.

"The succubus Nancy will bore your child. I know she will. She will bore the destroyer of mankind. He will be reign supreme lord over all Aryans. He will become the first patriarchy of the Asian-Aryan order."

...Tom was confused.

"What the hell are you talking about?"

This time, Tom couldn't take the phantom serious anymore.

The phantom put his hand down his own throat, to stretch out his actual head. His head popped up.

...It was Jake.

"Yo dude!" he said to Tom.

"...yo?"

...Jack was Jake this whole time?

"...dude, what the hell, what the fuck are you doing to me?" Tom said.

This time, Jake talked in a normal voice, and not in his haunted Jack voice with tons of reverb.

"Does this feel okay now? Hold on, let me change the environment. This is way too edgy."

With the snap of Jake's fingers, Tom and Jake were transported to a blank white zone. No sound, nothing. Just the two of them.

"What the fuck dude? I didn't know magic was fucking real? Who the fuck are you!?" Tom said.

"Sorry man, I'm Jake. ...No really. I am Jake. Jack is not my real name. Though Jack is what you thought I was."

Tom's skin was crawling.

"Well, okay dude, I could have been very formal about it, but, now that New York is being attacked, I had to come clean about myself. So like... I am apart of Satan's forces here to bring destruction to the Earth. ...Totally not in an evil way, but in a good way."

Tom's head turned.

"A good way, as in, everyone on this planet is a slimy Marxist sinner and I am here to cleanse the world of that shit and replace it with your ideology."

"...my ideology?"

"Yeah. You're the second coming of Jesus man."

Tom? The second coming of Jesus?

"So like, you basically the vision of the future. And what you're doing right now is the prophecy of the entire world. A new master race of Asian-Aryan people shall inherit the Earth and build a beautiful society, kind of like what you see in the art of Yoshitaka Amano or if you played any of those Final Fantasy games. Fun stuff like that. So I released the first horsemen from its grave and now it's attacking New York City. ...In order to start order, we have to destroy the major capitals of the world and get rid of those disgusting Je... I mean! ...*Jeww-deo*-Christian people and their corrupt sense of law!"

Tom looked amused.

Wait, why am I the second coming of Jesus? I'm just a normal guy. I didn't do anything wrong. Why am I special?"

"Because you had the first thought to assume Whites and Asians should come together as a collective! That is a no-no zone."

"Then who are you? Who's Nancy?"

"Nancy? She's really just some girl I wooed over. I used some of my satanic powers to woo her over."

"...But is she some kind of, thing, like you?"

Jake looked at his purple robe.

"No. Not really. She really is a normal girl with a hard upbringing. I think you should purse her dude."

"Wait, you know about what happened last night!?"

Jake turned his head.

"What happened?" he said.

...Guess he didn't know what happened last night.

"...never mind."

"All I am saying is that girl Nancy looks like she's more attracted to you then Daisy. She was having super fun last night. Maybe you should pursue her instead of Daisy. I will be honest, Daisy is kind of dependent on you and she's a little insecure. Nancy is strong and she can be a good mom... let me tell you!"

Now a satanic spirit was giving dating advice to Tom.

"No way. We just me, and, I don't want to break Daisy's heart and..."

"The prophecy will fulfilled if you fuck this girl. Have her child. The child will become the savior of mankind and the birth of Asian-Aryanism. I'm not kidding!"

"I can't leave Daisy!"

"But you could! She's nothing. Would you rather have a normal annoying hafu child, or a hafu child that saves mankind and transforms it into Gene Wolfe's The Book of

The New Sun? ...You should think about what you're
doing."

"But you're destroying New York City!"

"Who cares? Fuck New York. The West Coast is better
than the East Coast! Hot Asian girls everywhere!"

Tom and Jake now looking awkward as ever.

"Alright Tom, Nancy and Daisy are going to walk in the
house, and pretend nothing has happened, okay? Otherwise
I will use my powers and sedate you! Go and pursue
Nancy, okay?"

"But! But! But! The lizard thing that is destroying New
York! What about that."

Jake looked baffled.

"Oh yeah, that's true. Not this."

Jake raised his hands.

"Anyway! Go pursue your destiny Tom!"

The flashing blue absorbed all of Tom's his vision. His
was magically back on the sofa watching Star Vs. The
Forces of Evil.

Daisy and Nancy walked in the room.

"Hey, Tom!"

"Hi, ladies!" Tom said, without acknowledging
anything that just happened a few moments ago.

"Awesome! Everyone's back! I made Bagel Bites for
everyone!" Jake said, standing in the kitchen all happy!

"The beach is super fun Tom! We should go alone
together on a date!" Daisy said to Tom.

Tom smiled.

Everything was fine.

Nancy said to Tom, "Are we going to meet your long time internet friends tonight? That's going to be so cool!"

"Yes we are! I'm excited for you to meet them!"

Nancy had sand in green bra.

"Hold on, I got some sand in my titties."

She shook her tits up and down like a little kid.

"Let me go change and wash up first. Save me some bagels Jake!"

Tom looked over to Jake.

Jake made a magical wink.

…Tom was fucked.

12.

Night fell again. The city was quiet. Howard and Turtle came over around close to 9. Tom was confused. What should do about the prophetic vision he witnessed?

Tom watched cartoons until the gang came over. He tried to avoid the petty talk. He was out of it. Something was up.

Nancy and Daisy were becoming close friends. It was amazing this stranger entered Tom's life so soon. ...But what about Daisy. Tom loved Daisy more.

He got off from the coach to go get himself a beer from the fridge.

"Poor Tom, I didn't how sensitive he is to terrorist attacks. ...Especially by an alien," Turtle said.

"Aliens are real! Kek magic is real! Pepe is going to bless everyone!" Howard said jokingly.

"I mean, it wasn't dirty Muslim terrorist that destroyed the empire state building, it was a giant lizard creature. All the Pokémon nerds are going crazy for that one."

"That just proves aliens are real. And the monster went back into space like that. It came down to wreak havoc and went back up in space when it was done. ...I should have taken a picture of that thing."

Tom was drinking his beer in the kitchen.

"So, how about that? Monsters are real," Daisy smiled at Tom.

"Cheers!" he said. Hitting his bottle against Daisy's.

"Are you upset about what happened in New York?" she asked him.

"...Sort of. I kind of am. Monsters are real, who knew?"

"I'm amazed myself too. Glad it wasn't here.""

"Yeah."

Tom looking down on the ground like he had to say something more important.

"Alex Jones is right Howard. Take a look at what he's going to say this week. The Illuminati is real, Pizzagate is real, Esoteric Hitlerism is real, and meme magic is real! This is one crazy generation we are living in!" Turtle said.

"Yeah. The only thing is, I have to say, I am kind of happy New York got destroyed again. I don't know. I feel bad about the one guy I had on the podcast who loves New York City, but I love the idea of chaos and destruction. ...Do you think the monsters will come down from the heaven as an army and destroy the government? That way we can have a radical centrist government."

"Radical centrist? Anarcho-capitalism? No thanks. I like the ethno-state idea better. An ethno-state for everyone. Cool stuff like that," Turtle said.

Daisy joined in the conversation.

"You guys have to get on paranormal investigators on the show and talk more about occult things. That would mean everything about aliens are real!" she said.

"Wait, wasn't the creature green?" Howard asked.

Turtle looked at his phone. "I think he was."

"Are you thinking what I am thinking?"

"No, what are you thinking about?"

"...the creature was Pepe!"

Everyone was laughing.

Tom was alone in the kitchen. He thought of joining in with the bants of the crowd. Daisy might have thought Tom was a sensitive guy. He felt like going to bed. He headed upstairs. He didn't say word to the gang.

"Maybe the creature is a shit poster from mars and is getting revenge on all the norms who didn't believe nothing is possible!"

"No, it was like, the monster was mad at norms for trying to be cool..."

Howard and turtle speculated what the thing was.

Daisy was having fun drinking and talking to Tom's new friends.

Tom shut the door behind him and laid in his bed. ...Turns out Nancy was in the room calling someone.

"Yes Dad. I will be back soon. I with some friends right now. I will graduate from college. ...I will get a place. Ok."

She hung up the phone.

Tom and Daisy were now alone in a room together.

"Hi Nancy," Tom said to her unexpectedly.

"How did you get in here?"

"I don't know, I don't feel like having fun today. Kind of upset."

"About the monster thing? That is kind of cool."

"Not that, other things."

"Where's Jake?"

"Jake? I think he's hanging downstairs with the gang."

"Ok."

"Who was that on your phone?"

"My dad. We don't get along that much."

She sat beside the bed with Tom.

"He's too pushy on me. He wants me to be a Yamazaki just like my two older brothers."

"You're the only girl in the family?"

"Yeah."

"...what about your mom."

Nancy looked down on the bed.

"She divorce him. Too much. She's a model actually. She models for vogue and stuff like that. Shen ever understood the whole Japanese background thing at all."

"I see."

"And... My dad wants me to stay in school. But I want to live my life. I got all this money, and I don't know what I am spending it on."

Nancy sounded mopey.

"Really? You are a pretty girl, I don't understand why you don't have a boyfriend."

"Thank you. You're a handsome guy yourself."

This is the part where things were going to get truly awkward. He had to say it to her.

"Nancy. I had this strange last night, like I always do. And in this dream. I saw this phantom that told me that... that... supposedly, we are going to be together."

"Together?"

"Yeah, like dating."

Nancy giggled.

"What's that supposed to mean? Don't you have Daisy?"

"Daisy is great at all, but your different and, I don't know how to say this, but,"

Nancy had a smirk on her face.

"You like me. I know you do."

Tom felt embarrassed.

"Ok, yeah, I do. But there is more to it than that..."

"I like you to Tom. I feel better about myself when I am with you."

Tom fell silent.

"If you want, we can be friends with benefits and not tell a soul," she said with a whisper.

Tom felt somewhat aroused.

What I am really trying to say is, I had this crazy dream last night, and like, in this dream, you were going to have my baby."

"What? Your baby?"

"...Yeah, like I got you pregnant. And this kid was going to be the ruler of the world or something."

Nancy curled her finger into her fake hair.

"And you want to get married and have children that fast? Wow Tom, your making really quick moves on me! I like that!"

Tom started to blush.

"I'm serious. Nancy. We are going to have this half-White-Japanese kid and he's going to be like Donald Trump or something. And I had the choice between you or Daisy. And now I am torn up between the two?"

Daisy was laughing.

"...Are you high? I just popped some pills when I was on the beach with Daisy and everything is getting better today. I think you're doing something dude."

"No! Not at all. I am seeing things. We are like, going to have Asian-Aryan kids together and they are going to rule the world."

Nancy was laughing, she was getting closer to Tom.

"You know, Jake is just a friend. But you are different. I like guys like you. You're special."

Tom looked her in the eyes.

"I'm not so sure if I should have sex with you.

Nancy smiled, "why not? I have two day-after pills left. Fuck condoms!"

She laid down right next to Tom. Things were getting tense.

"...Nancy, I don't want Daisy to find out. I love Daisy as much as I love you. In fact, I don't know who I love anymore!"

Nancy rubber her nose on his neck.

"Tom, you know we are so much alike. You know that? You're going alone on an adventure. I was kicked out of my house. I have no one to hug. And... I am so desperate for someone to be with, like..."

Nancy started to tear up in one eyes.

"I want to be a mom too. I want a kid. It would be so nice."

Tom could not tell if Nancy was still high on drugs or if she really meant what she was saying. It was a mix of both.

"That's okay Nancy. Don't cry."

"No Tom. I like you a lot. I need you. I am begging to be apart what you do. You might think I am crazy... I have no place to go. I have no success. I am some lousy girl that everyone wants to use. Not you Tom. You're different!"

She said with some emotion in her tone.

"...Have you ever had a boyfriend Nancy?"

"Yes. They all sucked. All of them were abusive just like my family. I can't stand it anymore. I lost it. I don't care anything anymore. I want to live a good life. Not a shitty hooker life. You understand me, do you Tom?"

Tom probably talked to her the wrong time. Especially right after when she was talking to her dad.

"I understand. ...Nancy, I'm a virgin when it comes to sex. I only had my dick sucked... and like, you're the only the person that ever gave me a hand job... besides from that stupid girl Mary that did it to me when I was a teenager. My life is not that adventurous Nancy. I am a chaste person. You are a wonderful and badass person. You're super sexy and I like the way your tits bounce when you get sand of you."

Nancy smiled, wiping a tear from her face.

"Thanks. You cock is nice and is clean," she was laughing.

Tom was now holding her like baby. What was he doing? If Daisy walked in this room, that would be the end of their relationship.

"Hold on a second," Tom said.

He got up to lock the door.

He looked at Nancy laying on the bed.

"Nancy. I want to have a kid too. And, if you want to do something today, I am willing to stick my penis in a vagina for the first time in my life."

Nancy smiled.

"What's there a speech for? Just take off your clothes if you want to fuck."

Tom felt awkward.

Nancy was unbuttoning her pants and taking it down.

Tom did not know what to do.

138

13.

What the hell did he just do? …Tom had sex with a complete stranger.

That night, he cuddled with Nancy for a bit, and instead slept with Daisy. Daisy had no idea what was going on in that room with Tom and Nancy. Tom had to do it. Jake made him do it. His paranoia was getting to him.

Nancy liked it like nothing significant ever happened.

Tom sleep besides Daisy in the same bed. Still, he pretended he was shocked like a green lizard destroyed the empire state building. In reality, he cheated on Daisy.

…Why did he do such a thing? Is he an animal? Is Daisy not that good?

"Babe, let go and hang out on the beach tomorrow morning."

She said yes to that.

And that's exactly what they did the next day. Tom's face was dead with anxiety.

He was no longer in control of himself. He needed to hang around Daisy and only her.

Jake had to go do morning errands again. Though Jake now believes that the shapeshifter is lying and he and Nancy are playing a big joke on it.

Turtle and Howard left last night. Howard said he could hang out again tomorrow in the afternoon.

Tom and Daisy walked to the beach together for a nice bonding stroll. ...An important bonding stroll.

Daisy had on a summer hat with a sunflower on it. She wore a long pink dress. She looked like an honest and American Chinese mom. That's what Tom really wanted from her. ...Not that slutty Nancy.

Daisy Liang was the truth for Tom.

Tom walked with her holding her hands. He wanted to show how much of a good potential husband he can be. He was taller than her. She was short. Tom look good with his orange shit on. He didn't wearing his glasses today. He looked better without them.

"Tom, are you ok? You been acting strange lately."

"I've been trying to overcome everything that has been happening. I think I blew a 'funny fuse' or something. All this. Jake and Nancy, Howard and Turtle, and that extraterrestrial attack in New York... There is so much. I think I am having a writer's block."

Daisy looked back at Tom with the shadow of her hat covering her eyes.

"A writer's block? Is that all? You're sad because you have a writer's block?"

"...Yeah."

"Or is it something else I'm not aware of."

Tom got nervous.

"...Was it because that on night, me and Nancy were showing our titties and you think I am some kind of slut now, right?"

Tom didn't know what to say.

Daisy smiled.

"Well you can touch my tits whenever you want to Tom. You're the only person I like."

"...really?"

"Yes, really! Watch this!"

Daisy grabbed Tom's left arm and put it on her tit. She was wearing no bra.

She making his arm feel her left tit.

"See? It's not so bad!"

"Yeah," tom was laughing.

Daisy was only doing that cheer Tom up. Maybe Tom did think Daisy was a slut and that's why he's been quiet.

...Both got to the sand of the beach.

"This is where I and Nancy started our trek together. We went all the way down to the boardwalk? Want to go that way?"

"Sure. What did you guys do along the way?"

Tom and Daisy began walking on the beach. The sun was beaming as hot as ever. ...Tom should have put some sun screen on.

"I don't know, fun stuff. I learned a lot about her. ...It has nothing to do with me becoming a slut, ok?"

Tom nodded his head.

Daisy was kicking the sand as she walked.

"She's a really troubled girl. Her problems, you know."

Tom thought about the aggressive and abusive sex they had last night.

"I know..."

"Yeah. She is looking for a sister or someone to take care of her. She had no job, dropped out of college, and she does drugs and jerks guys off."

Tom was thinking to himself... "Yeah, I know."

"She needs to be sit on a good direction in life. We need to get her back to her family."

Tom looked surprised.

"We should!" he said.

"Huh?" she said back.

"We need to give her advice to go back to her parents and do the right thing. I would say she needs to become something more than a decadent person. Like, she needs to become a mom or a librarian, or some daycare nurse, anything to keep her out of trouble"

"Totally! I was thinking the same thing!"

Daisy looked right into Tom's eyes.

"...you're worried because Nancy is unstable? I understand. She made me nervous yesterday too. I hanged with your friends last night because I wanted to get away from her trauma."

Tom quickly nodded his head up and down.

"Exactly! You're exactly right! I don't think we can take care of her like her mom and dad. We need to give her direction and tell her to go back home!"

Daisy smiled.

"Mom and Dad? Imagine if we had a daughter and she was exactly like Nancy!"

Tom smiled too.

"You better step up your dad game. You need to make $60,000 a year, buy a place to live, and pay for our children's education!"

"Whhhaaa! Hold on their tiger mom! Why are you being picky?"

"I'm just saying, if we are going to have kids, you got to marry me and show some masculine values. I don't think you're going to make a fortune off of your white people comedy shows."

"Take that back!"

Daisy was teasing him. ...She likes him after all.

A Frisbee came flying over to the feet of Tom. A little Asian kid came over him. His hands were out reaching for the disc. Tom picked up the disc and gave it back to the kid.

"Thank you sir!" The little kid said to him.

Running back, his parents were there. A thinly build white dad and a fat and small Chinese wife waved back. Daisy waved back to them.

"Your kids are adorable!"

"Thanks! Have a nice day!"

"You too!"

...California was filled with White-male-Asian-female couples.

"Did you just see that family?"

"What?"

"That family?"

"I know! That's you and me in ten years!" she was laughing.

"Howard is right. This place is nothing but Asian-Aryanism on the beach and in the town!"

"...I think they were super cute. I feel so much better when I am around people like that."

"Really?"

"Yeah totally. I don't feel like the only Asian in the room ruled over by an obsessive white boyfriend. I feel like I belong to greater sense of meaning and purpose."

"Are you calling me obsessive?"

"Hell yeah. You wrote a whole book how much you want to bang Asian girls you per!"

She was laughing. Tom laughing too. Things look bright in their future.

There was a rock up ahead. "Let's sit down," she said to Tom.

Both took a sat on the rock looking out into the ocean. The sky had puffy white clouds. It looked like they were on a tropical island, but actually the dirty city was right behind them.

Daisy shook her sandals to get the sand out.

"...You think I can make a living as a teacher?" Tom said to her.

"I don't think that pays much."

"Your right. I thought about it. And all the black people I have to deal with."

"Yeah, screw that."

"I don't like teaching strangers either. I would rather be teaching my kids. I don't want to be pinned into being a teacher with my English degree either. I think I would rather work as a public relations agent."

"That sounds awesome. ...You had success on eBay, right?"

"Yes I did. If I had a commodity to sell all the time, I could be making $800 a week... I wish."

"...What is something you can get for something low, and then something you can sell for high?"

"Not sure. My brother would tell me stuff like that."

Daisy's phone was ringing. She had to answer it.

"Hello. ...Hi daddy! No, I am fine."

It was her Dad. Just like when Nancy's dad called her. Parents are always looking out for their kids.

...Daisy would speak English for a bit... until they changed up to a fierce and unintelligible and bug-like Chinese.

All Tom heard was, *"Cha-Cho-Chi La Do-fu-fer-neh-nana-serr."*

They way Daisy spoke Chinese was harsh and ugly. Compared to her cute and high pitched English. Her Chinese was deep and gurgle like.

"How-wa-so-fo-ka-ka-da-fer-niqua."

It was a nice day out...

"Tom, would like to talk to my dad?"

"Sure."

Tom only met the Dad once for tea. It was super formal and Daisy told him to make up stuff about his status to seem like a nice guy.

"Hello?"

An old sounding man was on the phone with a thick accent.

"Hello. Is this Thomas? How are you?"

"Good, how are you?"

"Good, is everything okay."

"Yes, everything is wonderful."

The simple conversation worked like that.

...Until Dad said something very strange.

"Will you marry my daughter? When is the wedding day?"

"Marry?"

"You are marrying my daughter, yes? What day is this?"

"Oh well..."

Looking at Daisy, he told the Dad,

"What date?"

"Next week? Yes? You will Marry her next week?"

"...Sure!"

Tom was out of his mind.

"We are going to get married, yes!" Tom said to her Dad.

"Good, may I speak to Biyu?"

Her past the phone back to Daisy.

"Married, did you say married?" she said back to Tom.

"Yeah. Married. We are getting married in a week."

The Chinese started up again on the phone. This time, Daisy's Chinese was loud and aggressive.

"BO-BO-BAHWADERA!"

She said goodbye to her Dad after a few more minutes.

"...You told my dad were getting married next week?"

"Yeah. I wanted to make sure that happened so he's not worried that I plan on taking an advantage of you."

Daisy was shocked.

"We are not even in Pennsylvania and we have limited money. How the hell are we supposed to get married in a week and see my parents again?"

"...Don't we have a gig in Las Vegas tonight?"

"Didn't you say you would skip that to spend a week at Jake's house?"

"I did. But with Nancy's pleading for help and Jake's warm welcoming, I think it's important we leave around 3PM and ShowTime at 11PM. We will get a hotel and find a church tomorrow."

"Shotgun wedding? That is so American of you! What about the big expensive wedding?"

"We can do that to later on! Let's make it official first and getting married tomorrow."

Daisy couldn't believe what she was hearing. Tom was acting so dull today, and now he's popping the question. That's why he was so quiet.

"...Well... That sounds awesome Tom. I love you too." She smiled.

"Haha, I didn't ask you will you marry me or get you a ring. I can do that next week when we are back in Pennsylvania."

"...Let's go right now!"

"What?"

"Let's go now! IT's such a beautiful day today! Tell Jake and Howard we are leaving and getting married. Let's celebrate tonight after your skit! ...Call your going in for the Vegas show."

Daisy took Tom's hand and starting rushing back to the house.

"Hold on babe, not so fast!"

She was laughing and twirling around.

Tom came in for a long kiss with her.

Her fat fell off and rolled over the sand.

...Quickly getting back to the house, Tom told Howard and Jake that he, Daisy and Nancy had to catch a stand-up show in Las Vegas. He didn't tell Jake that they planned on getting married, but hinted to Howard that he was.

Packing up everything in the car, Jake harassed Tom for a bit.

"Remember Tom. You're going to have a good future ahead of you. I hope you know what you're doing and take care of Nancy. She's a really good girl."

"Then you should take care of her."

"No, we will certainly meet up again in the future! I think she should be a radio and look out for you. Especially the point that she is a good caretaker! Win! Wink!"

The spirit of Jake was showing against Tom. Tom knew Jake wanted him to get with Nancy. Hopefully, Nancy did take her birth control pills this morning.

Nancy was quite excited to go an adventure again.

"Wow Jake! I can't believe you're going to Las Vegas and brining me with you!"

"Are you sure you don't want to stay with Jake?"

"I think Jake is fine with me going with you, aren't we going be meeting him again soon?"

"Yeah, we will." Tom was being a little sarcastic.

Howard shook Tom's hand goodbye and told him he should start doing the co-host position again in two weeks.

The cat was already packed and everything was ready to go. ...That quick. Daisy knew Tom had never missed a stand-up. The whole proposal violated both Tom and Daisy. Nancy came for the adventure and for Tom.

In the car, Tom wished Jake one final goodbye.

"Jake, Please. Don't send anymore fucking monsters onto this planet! Everything is under control and I will fulfill what you told me to do," he said with a whisper.

150

"That's good to hear. I think she is under your spell," Jake said.

Everything went by so fast. They were on road again leaving Santa Barbara.

...How quickly time flies.

14.

The crew was already on the road again. 3PM and on that dirty highway. Route X going nowhere, eventually leading to Las Vegas. Tom was driving, Daisy in the front seat, Nancy in the back. They listening to Mitski for the billionth time.

"I really like this album. I wish she would go on tour again," Daisy.

"I saw her at the Church in Philly. She's okay. She like, read my book before it was ever published. She said it was 'keeewwl.' I don't know," Tom said.

"This is some cute stuff," Nancy said in the back.

Tom was getting annoying.

"If there were not two girls in the car, I would gladly put on some Digital Hardcore. Like The Shizit, or Bastards United, loud harsh stuff like that..."

"Don't put that on now," Daisy said.

The GPS spoke, "30-more-miles-till-destination,-turn-right-on-exit-25,-on-right."

Nancy was curious, "so what do you have plan to speak of tonight?"

Tom thought about it.

"Not to sound cliché, but nothing really. I'm like Seinfeld. I like to talk about nothing, but possibly about Asian girls and all that jazz."

"Really? Is that the only thing you're going to talk about?"

"Well... I mean, there was a lot of stuff happening the last two days. I have material."

...Like if Nancy was trying to say something to Tom.

"You should talk about your friends from Santa Barbara!" Daisy said.

"Or what about us getting drunk and playing Cosmic Encounter!" Nancy said.

Tom took all those things into consideration.

"Yeah, yeah. That sounds super fun...."

Tom was concentrating on the road.

"Nancy, what are you going to do when we are done the tour? We plan on heading back to Pennsylvania after tonight's show?" Daisy asked.

"Not sure... I don't know where I am going to go."

"Didn't you take an Uber all the way to see us?"

"Yeah. But I was hanging out with some shifty guys as a roadie. And I didn't want to deal with them anymore. So I planned to meet with Jake instead. Personally, I am thinking about staying with you guys, if you care about that."

Tom thought about what she said.

"Nancy. I think you should go live with her your parents again."

"...Hell no, why would I want to do that?"

"You need protection and we are also settling down near Philly too. We will all be close to one another."

"No way. I want to stay with you guys."

Tom didn't tell the truth yet to Nancy. But he had to.

"Nancy, I have to tell you this, but me and Daisy are getting married."

Daisy blushed.

"What?"

"We are getting married this week and then we are moving back to Philly. We will be living together."

"No way," she said.

"Yes we are. So, we want to plan that out and have time together."

Nancy was somewhat upset what she was hearing. She jerked his dick off last night and all of a sudden the guy is getting married? Obviously he's too scared to propose to Nancy.

"Like, did you know about this?" she looked at Daisy.

"No! I did not. I had no idea Tom would propose to me like this. It was so sudden."

...And he didn't propose to Nancy.

"Really? Tom, you make quick moves," she told him.

Tom had to tell the truth.

A pit stop was ahead only five minutes away.

"Well, what do you think about that girl Suzy, huh? Him going out with that Jack!?"

Nancy was teasing Tom.

Tom was getting nervous. "Jack who?"

"Jack Marston and Suzy Wang. You know those two. In fact, I think you had a crush on her too!"

Tom was trying not to get ma. He had to pay attention to the road.

"Hold on. I need to go to the pit stop to take a leak and get food."

"Does Daisy know about Jack and Suzy?"

Daisy looked on the ground.

"Yeah, he told me how much he had a crush on her and how he had disturbing revenge fantasies against Jack. How did you know Suzy?"

"We were like best friends in college. Jack was a smart guy. President of the game club, kind of nerdy, handsome looking, and all the Asian girls wanted him. I remember they would all go up to him because he was the white guy everyone wanted to be with."

Tom had burning anger against Mary, who only joined the game club because of Jack. ...At least he got a hand job from her. He was getting mad.

"I fucking hate those kids Nancy, don't bring them up," he said.

"Well it's obviously your whole book is anger towards the norms with Asian girlfriends and your men-going-their-own-way hatred towards Asian women, isn't that true?"

"No it's not! I love Asian women and I hate men who abuse them!"

"Sounds to me someone has college trauma and dwells on the past of being a loser," Nancy was being bratty.

"I don't give a shit what Jack and Suzy do every day or after college. I hope they are not together anymore..."

"I bet you think about Suzy every day and wish you could have had her as a girlfriend. You wish you could have had somebody to cuddle and kiss your everyday before you went in on morning classes Monday, Wednesday, and Friday. Someone to sit down and talk to you ate Lunch at noon every Tuesdays and Thursday and play free board games. Nothing to think about but your Asian slut and desires coming true! ...I bet you saw Jack slobber all over Suzy every morning too and you were burning with anger. And you hated him for that want. And you probably had thoughts of shooting up the school too!"

"Stop teasing him Nancy. Tom is super sensitive to issues like that. He's trying to overcome his trauma," Daisy interrupted.

"Well you try to be one of the only white guys on an all-girls school campus and try to woo over the Asians. All the white girls were bitchy blue haired feminist and the Asian girls all gravitated towards Jack. I didn't have any of them because they were not interested in me even when I tried to be with them! I started the fucking board game club way before that asshat Jack started it! And I started the whole Chinese club even before the Chinese came into the school. And that motherfucker took everything from me!"

Jack was getting mad.

The pit stop was on the left. Jack turned onto the left.

The GPS spoke, "Recalculating!"

"I don't think we should talk about this," Daisy said.

"Seriously, watch out Daisy. Don't let Tom marry you for the sake that he is fulfilling some trauma he could never get over. Don't be a pawn to his game."

Nancy was being harsh on Tom.

Tom didn't say anything. He was mad. If he did say something, Nancy could talk about last night.

Tom parked outside the pit stop.

"Let me go to the bathroom and get some food first."

"Alright, me too," Nancy said.

Daisy soon followed.

The gang walked into the pit stop. Tom head straight to the bathroom. Daisy went her own direction. Nancy followed Tom.

Tom was washing up in the men's bathroom. Nancy knew his secrets. Was she some kind of phantom like Jake was? How was Jake a spiritual phantom of Jack? Did he make up Jake? Is Nancy some kind of devil spirit like Jake? Is she Suzy? Tom better watch what he says in front of Daisy. And what he says in front of her too.

Nobody was in the bathroom. He was alone. Washing his hands after his leak, he thought about how he could push Nancy back home and be quiet about his marriage.

Things had to go his way. It's like he picked up a spoil brat out of nowhere.

...That's when Nancy walked in the guy's bathroom.

"Nancy? Why are you hear? This is the guy's bathroom?"

"I want to talk to you," she said.

Nancy stared at him. Alone in the room.

"Do you love me?" She said to him.

"I... I... Look, last night was super strange. I did say it because you caught in me..."

"I know you do," she said.

"..You're very pretty and I do like you. But I was with Daisy longer. ...Do you know about Jake being a spirit?"

"Being what?"

"A spirit! I tried to tell you this last night. He wanted me to get you pregnant so we have child together and this child will save the world. The lizard thing that attacked New York yesterday... That was Jake's doing. He's behind."

Nancy turned her head.

"That sounds fucking crazy, but you make somewhat sense."

"Jake is basically Jack. Jack is haunting me every day. He's not just a mortal person anymore. He's a spirit I created and now is this... satanic monster that wants me to live this fantasy upon the world. I don't know what to do!"

Tom sounded serious. Nancy thought he was confused.

"I'm staying at this pit stop, go on without me."

"What?"

158

"I don't need to hitch with you guys to Las Vegas. I can call an Uber and they can take me to a Bus depot. I would rather go home by myself. I have to settle down myself."

"What? What do you mean?"

"Yes, I'm serious. If I did it to meet you guys, I can do it on my own. I don't need to see you guys get married. I don't need to see that."

Tom was feeling sympathetic.

"Nancy. I am not mad at you. I love you as a friend and love Daisy. I can't love you both. I want to have a family and kids. You should do the same too."

She looked right at him.

"Tom, I'm having the baby. I'm going to fulfill your wildest nightmare. I will not tell Daisy it's yours and will not interfere with you. I will get home as soon as possible and prepare for it. I'm going to be a good mother."

Tom was shocked. She was having it.

"Alright... he said. That's ok with me. I love you and the child. I love you both. I can't break up with Daisy and be with you. I have to be with her too."

Nancy smiled, "then I am your secret second wife. I won't tell Daisy it's your baby and I will keep it a secret. I will keep that promise, agree?"

She forced out her hand looking for a shake.

Tom was nervous to shake it.

"You better not tell a soul!"

Tom shook her hand.

He then kissed her on the cheek.

"I love you Tom... I'm going. Tell Daisy I love her too. Let's meet up again when I have the baby!"

She suddenly left the bathroom.

"Nancy, do you have everything? Are you okay?"

"Trust me Tom, I will be fine!"

She left the guys bathroom unapologetically. She was about to catch an Uber to some unknown destination.

...This was going to be hard to tell this to Daisy.

Daisy left Tom like that.

And then he forgot to say, "I love you," one final too.

15.

Nirvana was an exotic place. It was between Heaven and hell and right next to Limbo. Jake was rushing across the lines of Limbo, in order that he talk to one of the higher ups in Limbo.

There in Limbo sat Buddha, big and grand. He was meditating in a deep sleep.

"Buddha! Buddha oh great Buddha! I have important news for you!"

Buddha was deep in concentration and did not want to be bothered.

"Buddha wake up! It's me! Jake T'choliz'chka!"

Buddha opened his right eye.

"The power of Satan, what information do you bother me with?" he said in a grand booming voice.

"The prophecy is going to be fulfilled! On the mortal earth, I tricked the mortal called Tom Deluge into marriage with a girl named Nancy Yamazaki. Together they will have a baby that will start the Kali Yuga!"

"...But who bring an end to it?"

Jake thought about it for a second.

"But... The offspring of Jake and Nancy will start the new era!"

"People suffer every day, but they do not need to suffer into black nihilism. Satan... you told me you would help benefit the cause of the woke one, not your selfish desires."

Jake was at a loss of words.

"But I! But I! But I am being told by my boss to do these things! I have no purpose living in the mortal world. I was created by the imagination of the mortal Tom, who will bring about the ending days of Earth!"

Buddha was angry.

"You have sent the Leviathan onto Earth and have caused much damage. I did not ask for that. Let the human beings know that in twenty-five years, Judgement day will come. They will be judge by each of their actions and be sent to Limbo. As for the rest of the people, they will become a part of the new society Tom's offspring will create!"

Jake did not know what to say.

"Mighty magnificent Buddha. I am sorry I cause you distress. I hope the world will be safe in the coming decades."

Jake left the golden room of the great Buddha.

He was angry.

"Fuck! How come I didn't get my fair share of seventy virgins he promised!? I don't care for the mortal life at all!

I'm just doing my job! I hope the boss doesn't get mad at me for this."

An angel named Gabriel came approaching Jake.

"Brother Jake, what seems to be the problem? Have you talked to Buddha today?"

"Yes I have. I was not rewarded for what the Buddha told me to do. I was only following orders from my boss Satan that mortal should get with the wrong woman to have the rebirth of Lucifer."

"Who might that mortal be?"

"Some young kid named Tom Deluge. I was a mortal on Earth a bit and seduced to Nancy Yamazaki, the new mother of Lucifer."

"Let's me see where they are now.

Gabriel create a giant glowing orb of golden power, showing the Milky Way and all living creatures at once in a vortex. Only Gabriel could see through this magnificent ball of destiny.

"...The mortal you speak of, Tom, he will have four children."

"...Wait! Four children?"

"Yes... Three from his wife, Daisy Liang and one from his widow, Nancy Yamazaki."

The prophecy was going to be fulfilled! However, three children from Daisy?

"How do you know this Gabriel?"

"I can read through destiny. This is what is going to happen Jake."

"...Would that mean one child of Daisy's offspring will as being a messenger too?"

"Yes, the first born child will be!"

...Jake was in serious trouble now. One message will be born from Nancy, and the other from Daisy.

"Wait, how does that even work? I thought there was only supposed to be ONE messenger, not two!"

"God made it that way that there are two now."

...How the hell is Satan going to hear this bad news?

***

...Back on Earth, Tom was about to perform his skit in a Las Vegas Casino.

"Give a warm round applause for Tom Deluge!!"

A room more than 100 people were clapping. Tom was opening up for a bigger comedian.

"Go Tom!" Daisy was yelling in the crowd,

Tom stepped on stage waving to everybody. He wore geeky blue shoes and a really bad Sonic Youth shirt. He shaved right before the show to show off his faded mustache. He wore glasses for the geek effect.

"Hey! How it's going everyone? What's up?"

The crowd roared.

Tom started to roar too.

"Tom Green use to do that too when he did comedy, RAAAAWWWWRRR!!!"

Tom sounded so retarded.

"So guys, let me tell you the fucking crazy week I had. Not only did I drink and bang tons of Asian chicks... just kidding... I had this strange dream. Did you know I am the prophet that will save this Earth? My children are going to lead a political revolution and stop the world from the green fucking thing that came smashing New York City... by the way, I feel super bad for everyone that died that day... but anyway... no serious, I was drunk and I smoked weed for the first time, and I was like... my children are going to save the world!"

Everyone was laughing. Daisy was laughing too.

"Maybe I am just taking this thing way too far. I just proposed to my girlfriend Daisy Liang and now she is my fiancée, and she is here tonight. She's right over there." Tom was pointing at her.

Everyone was clapping and cheering.

Daisy was excited and flattered. She was Tom's wife now.

"But that's why I am getting all paranoid and crazy. With a last name like Liang... guys, my wife Chinese... and my children are going to be like Elliot Rodger."

Everyone burst out laughing. Daisy laughing too.

"My children are going to shoot up the school the first time they enter kindergarten! My children are going to bitch about being white and cry like fat social justice warriors. If they do any of that shit they are going to get a traditional Irish paddle-whack from me! I don't want any of that shit in my house. Also, they are going to learn to love white people. God bless people like Gavin McInnes for going out to college campuses and fighting for white America! Fuck yeah!"

Everyone was going crazy and clapping their hands.

"But anyway, I don't care what my children are going to be... but if I have daughters, they will be the most beautiful looking things ever. Seriously, Eurasian women are everything. If you a little Eurasian guy, chances are you're going to shoot up the school and be a little Yukio Mishima. Which of course, I am all for. In fact I hope of a son so he can be the next Yukio Mishima and show the world he can run it. I'm tired of all that weak gay shit half-Asian men stand for. They are fucking white and should be proud to be white!"

Tonight, Tom was controlling the crowd with his brand of Asian-Aryan humor.

Daisy was clapping and smiling. This was his guy that loved him. Tom inside was a sensitive guy that didn't mean what he said. He's just like Daisy in this world. Looking for someone to be with, to have meaning, and to have greater purpose. Daisy turned into a full believer of Asian-Aryanism.

16.

...Many months later, Tom and Daisy moved outside of Philadelphia. Daisy's Dad was happy about their sudden marriage. He was too culturally naive to understand it was a shotgun marriage or had any concern about life between Tom and Daisy. Tom decided to get a job as a cashier at a comic shop he loved. The comic shop was on the mainline of Philadelphia, so the income was quite good for a simple job. Daisy was already in labor. Tom was going to be a dad soon enough. For not, the job at the comic store supplied the extra cash they needed to pay on the rent. Both had enough money to buy a house nearby. For now, they lived at a small space together in Manayunk.

Tom did not hear back from Nancy. However, he has been doing three podcast a week with Howard and keeps in touch on the Alt-Twee discord.

Tom thought about writing a second book, but could not feel like he should. He wanted to pay attention making money and being a good husband. Life was going good for Tom.

What was even more exciting is that Tom was working in a store that featured not only comic books but board games. Tom loves board games. He could tell any customer about the game, its origin, how it's played, the same way a librarian focuses on book subjects.

Tom cared more about board games then he did comics.

As for comics, Tom was into the super tween stuff, like *Bee and Puppycat, The Lumberjanes, Gotham Academy, Teen Dog, Plutona*, anything that reminded him of his own brand of Asian-Aryanism.

But he also loved the classical edgy stuff, from the English comic artist to the bleak manga artist.

Tom knew about everything in the store. He was a master of his own domain.

The manager only came in on Mondays and Wednesdays. He was already making enough money from the store to support his own decadent and isolated hobbies. The manager had a million days off. Tom wanted to be around things he liked. ...he didn't care if the customer got anything. He liked being paid by the hour doing nothing.

...But there was that one day Tom had a changing perspective about his future and his own art.

No one usually came in the store. It was on Wednesday, comic book day, did the old time collectors came in to buy comics to collect. Tom was aware of the rarity of each comic pressed and tried to make future predictions which one would sell. Tom never read comics for story lines. He saw single issue comics as collector items to resell in the future.

But on one of these Wednesdays, there was a girl looking around the board game section by herself.

She had black hair and huge Wayfarers. From the back of her head, you could tell she was Asian.

That same aisle, Tom was organizing leftover comics of *Snot Girl*, a comic that no one ever bought.

She looked like she was aimlessly bored, doing nothing.

Tom had to ask the default robot question any boring clerk would ask.

"Are you looking for anything in particular?" he said.

She looked back at him.

"Umm... do you know where the Mega Man comics are?"

Tom organized all the back issues in alphabetical order. If he was in "S," then Tom had to go right.

Passing her by to find the comic, Tom's heart rushed. This girl was too familiar. It was reminding him of a certain trauma that was buried deep in himself. Passing her by, he found the comics.

"They are right here!"

"Thank you!" she said in a quiet voice.

There was an open window for conversation. She looked all too familiar... Tom had to ask her.

"Hey, wait, were you in my Social Justice class? The one with Mr. Murphy?"

She looked dumbfounded.

"Yes, who are you?"

"Oh, I'm Tom! I sat at the other side of the table. You sat between two of those petty girls that were like, the teacher's pet," he laughed.

"Oh really? Wait, I think I do recall. You talked about *Neuromancer*, right?"

"Yes! The one time about Margaret Atwood and her strange book that reminded of it. That was a hard book."

"Oh wait, I recall you now. I don't remember you wearing a mustache at all!"

"No, ha, that was two years ago, wasn't it?"

"So you have always worked at the comic store?"

"It's only been three months. I'm married now and I am going to be having a kid soon."

The girl was shocked,

"Really? You're going to have a kid? That's amazing!"

"Yeah, so, a job about comics and board games, that's what pays the bills at the moment!" Tom was laughing.

Tom forgot the girl's name. He had to ask her.

"I'm sorry, what is your name?"

The girl replied, "I'm Suzy."

Suzy... That was it.

"Ok yeah, I was in the game club for a bit too at the club, and you were, hanging out with that one kid... what's his name, the guy with the brown hair, Sailor moon t-shirt, purple jeans..."

"Jack? Oh Jack, yeah he was my boyfriend."

Tom's blood was rushing.

"Yeah, yeah, yeah. I saw you guys together always at every classroom, you know, kissing each other like that."

Suzy was laughing.

"Yeah, well, that was years ago. We are friends now. I mean, I liked him. But we are no longer together at the moment."

Tom looked down on the ground, "I see."

He had to change the subject from getting his trauma out.

"So, are you into acting? I remember you liked that stuff?"

"Acting? How did you know I was in the Jester club?"

Tom was kind of a stalker when it came to his crushes.

"Well, I saw you perform once at the auditorium. Did you still act? You look like Madison Hu or maybe Haley Tju if you brush your hair in a certain way."

Suzy was laughing.

"Thank you so much! I always wanted to be an actor. By now I work at restaurant as a waitress!"

"Well we all have goals, I released book and went on a comedy tour."

"Really?"

"Oh yeah, I do comedy!"

"Is it bad or dirty?"

"Uh... No, it's really personal stuff."

Tom was looking directly at Suzy in a strange way.

"That's so cool, can I look you up on google?"

"Yeah sure, just write my full name, Tom Deluge..."

Tom and Suzy were already having fun reconnecting with one another and sharing social network sites. And as well exchanging text numbers.

"That is so cool you are doing all of this after college. I still don't know if I want to go to grad school. My parents are pushing me to do it."

Tom scratched his own back.

"...So you like The Mega Man comics? I find the funny. I like the sonic comics that gives me nostalgic feels of the past."

"Oh yeah. I like Mega Man. I think he's super cool."

"And I remember you like Pikachu too! Pokémon? I remember you had those stickers all over your laptop during social justice classes."

"Haha! You remember that? Wow, that's some time ago. I didn't know I was that popular. Why didn't we hang out at all?"

"I don't know. I was going through my own thing, I had homework, and you had a boyfriend too..."

Tom was feeling awkward.

"Oh I see. Well, that was the past. Things are different today."

Suzy was heading towards the cashier. Tom followed her there.

"Do you like board games too?"

"I was going to pick up this interesting game called Flux. I played the Batman version at my friend's house and quite like it."

"Flux? Oh yeah. I talked to the guy on my podcast. He's really cool. You should try out his latest release, Pyramid Arcade. That is totally out there."

"You have a podcast too? That is so cool!"

Tom felt like a muscular man showing off his abs.

"Well, yeah, I had many famous people on the show. I was doing since my senior year."

Suzy was impressed.

"That is so cool! We have to hangout sometime."

Tom felt a little nervous.

"...Hey, do you know a girl named Nancy?"

"...Nancy?"

"Yeah, Nancy, were good friends."

Suzy got all excited.

"Nancy!? Get out! I haven't seen Nancy since college!"

"Yeah, she came along as a roadie for my comedy tour. She is super supportive and remembers you!"

"Do you still hang with her?"

Tom didn't know what to say.

"No... But, I can call her over at my house and you should come over, and we can play like, board games."

"Totally! This is so exciting! I can't believe you know Nancy!"

Tom couldn't believe he knew Nancy either.

"Yeah well... Its Asian central over at my house. My wife is Chinese, Nancy is Japanese..."

"Really? That's so funny!" Suzy now laughing.

"Yeah, I guess it's something that doesn't leave you as a teen."

"That is totally awesome. You and Jack would have been best friends back then!"

...they could have been. Maybe.

"Yeah..."

Tom scanned in the comic of Mega Man and Suzy gave him the cash. He gave the change back.

"Well it's so cool to meet up with you! What are you doing this week?"

"Nothing much. At home with Daisy. You should come over."

"Sounds like a plan, later Tom! Nice talking to you!"

She waved at him as she left the store.

...The girl. The girl that teased Tom forever now wanted to get to know it.

...It was too late. He has an Asian girl on his own.

Tom felt his blood rushing throughout his body. That's all he ever wanted to hear in his college years. A sense of belonging.

And I'm sitting in Shakespeare's garden,
underneath a tree.
Wishing that my missing angel
could come back to me
To help me breathe.

-Cause & Effect

THE RAPE OF M'KHAL

1.

Destruction. Blood. A building collapse. A war-torn alien planet. Bullets fire in one direction. Pillaged by the human race. —The Sarparians!

The exotic alien planet was in the way of the Imperium. The great "Imperium" once predicted by a man named Francis Parker Yockey. —The Imperium of mankind. It's mission was to unite the stars together. To destroy all threats against humanity. This planet was next in line.

The race known to inhabit the home world of Mowo were called the Midorai. A green skinned, white haired, slit eyed, dog-nose, cat paw and tail creature that looked to much like a certain race of Sarparian beings. They were first discovered by the Asian-Aryans in 4020. Twenty years later, the capital of Mohawii was under siege by the Imperium.

The Midorai council refused to join the galactic, globalized powers. The anti-semitic and nordic space-vikings, known as the Sarparians, attacked the capital.

Destruction. Blood. Everything falling down, like that of the great virgin city of Dresden.

Some Sarparians were drafted to the war by force. The Sarparians believed that humanity could only unite the "pure" blood race of their ancestors, the Odins. The Odins were tall, blonde, blue-eyed germanic people of the past. Their great prophet and leader was Eduf Hattler. Once hated years ago, his party was resurrected, and the sins of Judeo-Christian culture was purged from Terra. The world was under multiple parties of humanity. The Sarparians were the elitist party that would leave their home system of the milky way, and venture into new galaxies. Either the foreign alien species would join them (from the prophecies told by the great Hattler), or they will suffer greatly.

The Midorai, once preserved by the Asian-Aryan sect of humanity, has now fallen under the hands of The Sarparians. Their destruction began.

Sarparian soldiers wore blue metal suits. Engraved were holy symbols of the swastika. Birth, Life, Death, Rebirth. All for the great Hattler. The Midorai to them were scum. They could do whatever they wanted to do to them. Kill them. Throw the babies into the fire. Fuck them.

That's what Johov was going to do.

Johov is an angry, disoriented Sarparian of the future. He has no parents. He was raised by the Information Society. A cow pumped up with artificial chemicals to make him a warrior. He has no direction in life. His only purpose was to kill.

His arms clenched the trigger of his guns and he shoots rounds of bullets at the innocent bystanders of the green race.

The Midorai have no stable army. They never learned how to defend themselves.

Johvo was to separate and go into a different direction. His mission was simple. —Wipe out the green bastards until he was called back to the launch pad.

Spraying bullets as he moved forward. Explosions. Louder than anything.

This world would be finally nuked after the carnage.

The purpose was to enslave the Midorai and turn them under galactic rule.

The children of the Midorai ran everywhere. Under rocks and inside buildings. There was nowhere to hide. Each was waiting for a bullet to race through their heads.

Any second now.

Johov had to search and destroy every single one of them. He could not find any one in sight.

He entered a tower that reached the tip of the orange sky. He was looking for animals to butcher.

Still, nothing in sight.

Johov shot a round of bullets at the wall. Then, he was out of ammo. Nothing to shoot at anymore. He could recharge his gun, or switch to an even more deadly weapon.

He heard an alien "yelp" of some kind coming from the other room. He wanted to find the thing and let it cry in front of him.

Walking to left, the noise was louder. It sounded like a cat mixed with the cry of a human. A "Nyannyannyan" sound.

There was the creature.

It's leg was broken. On the floor, crying. No one else was in the room.

Now it was Johov and the thing. Johov look straight at the thing in pain.

Messy white hair, green skin... naked. Her tits were showing. It was a woman.

Johov felt a sense of nostalgia. The Midorai looked exactly liked a Sarparian.

Angry, he could just kill the thing right now. Make it's head explode. Kick it until it dies.

On the other hand, Johov and a sick perversion.

Sarparian soldiers never had the chance to reproduce until they were proven "worthy." The Sarparian women were blonde valkyrie that would work in the wheat fields, take care of the children, run academia, and were the keeper of the arts. It was the men who had to suffer.

In fact, Sarparian marriage is arranged. It is not in the free will of the Sarparian to find himself another Sarparian woman. Sarparian woman are known to be rude, selfish, and bipolar. It took an certain attitude to have sex with one. An attitude to be proven "worthy."

Johov, 25 years of age, never had sex in his life. It was told by propaganda in Sarparian society that sex was only for "the golden ones." The ones who deserved. The ones who took the iron pill and master the "game" magic.

Johov's mind was cruel. He hated women.

Seeing this alien creature cry for help made him more angry. He saw tears flowing down her eyes.

This is it. This is where Johov could rape this thing and dominate it. To make sense out of his abusive life.

The Midorai woman laid on ground, begging for help. A shadow cast over her.

She had nice tits. Plump and natural. Her waist and legs were like a cheetah's. Exotic, but very human like.

Johov clenched his teeth.

She screamed again, "Nyannyannyan!"

Johov put down his gun.

"Shut up you fucking bitch!" He yelled at it.

She looked back at him. Tears falling from her eyes.

"Nyanyah!" she yelled back. Like a siamese cat talking back to it's owner. She yelped a couple more times.

Johov felt anger. He could kill her. It wasn't worth it.

No one was inside. It was a dark room. Him and her.

Johov grabbed both of her arms. He looked down at her dress. It was torn up. He could easily slide down her alien skirt.

It was easy for Johov to take off his pants, his ultra marine metal pants. He could easily eject the zipper pocket and get his penis out.

Johov laid the creature on the ground. She moved her head back and forth, like she was waving "No." Her zebra like-legs curled up to her waist.

"You motherfucker you!" He yelled at it. Johov was wrestling with the creature. He wanted to suck the thing's tits.

His helmet was off, and soon enough, he was sucking on her nipples. It was exactly like how Sarparian tits should feel. Not hard, but soft skin that feels like he could drink milk from it. Johov's saliva dripped all over her green skin.

He tightly hold down both of her arms. She could not move because of Johov pinning down her legs.

The creature had her slit eyes and mouth closed. She didn't know what was going on. She didn't resist.

Johov wanted to rape the shit out of this animal.

He thought about it. Was he committing an act of bestiality? A species that cannot reproduce with one another. He was going to ejaculate on this animal, but where?

Instead of sucking the tits, he reached for her face. She was afraid to look at him. Johov licked and ate her face. He bite her Sarparian-like lips. She was yelping with more "Nyans."

The Nyans were arousing Johov.

She kept closing her mouth. Johov's tongue followed her month whenever she opened it. He finally was able to reach the tongue inside of it.

The Midorai tongue felt like a lizard's tongue. Long and sexy. She had teeth like a cat. It felt so Sarparian.

Soon, the woman was falling for Johov's motion. Her mouth open and her tongue dodging the un-expected tongue of his. Her eyes still closed. She thought that this alien was planting eggs inside her. This alien was incredibly submissive. Almost romantic.

...Do the Midorai even know what the concept of "rape" is?

Johov's legs were pinning down her legs. Now he was full on humping her.

Johov's flipped out his dick. He put his arm around her mouth and he inspected her legs using the forehead of his penis.

"Where the hell is this thing's vagina?," he asked.

Johov violently ripped her dressed, stripping her fully naked. That, while he was biting her belly like a wolf taking down a sheep.

Johov grabbed her legs. He found a furry sideways hole between the legs. It looked like the anus and the vagina was just a single hole. Why not? That's where the fucking is.

Johov turned the creature sideways. Her obnoxious butt rubbed on his chest. Johov was horny. He felt like he was in some kind of ultra porno. He grabbed his dick, measured it with her hole, and inserted his penis insider her. She was getting too weak to make any noises. They were now just cute murmurs.

Johov's put his penis inside of her like pencil sticking inside a pencil sharpener. He could feel the soft anus tissue of the alien. Like rubber walls.

He was violently pushing against her. Her ass smacking against his swastika coat. Her sexy sideways position felt like she was actually consenting his invading dick.

His 7-inch dick felt nice inside an animal vagina, even if this was considered "bestiality."

Johov was insane.

Taking his dick out, sperm oozed from the tip to her little hole. He painted the sperm on her round ass like an artist.

Johov smacked his dick on her ass. Put it back inside of her again. She didn't make any noise this time.

Johov grabbed her titties. How soft they felt! How better they were than the Sarparian women he hated.

Johov had another twisted thought:

"Why don't I brand this bitch and make her my sex slave? Hell yeah. I can fuck her every time I kill some worthless people!"

He smacked her ass again out of this happy thought.

Johov yelled at her,

"Look at me! Look at me you dumb cunt!" Look!"

She didn't understand what he was saying. Her eyes and mouth closed, tears falling from her. soaking into her own puddle, escaping from his presence.

He reached out and gently moved her white hair from the side. He looked directly into her cute, slit eyes.

"Listen bitch! Your going to be my fucking whore! I'm going to fuck you all the time!"

She said nothing.

Johov could kill her right now if he wanted too. He didn't want it. She had a fine ass and a nice pair of alien titties. He rolled her around to look at her belly. He started inserting his dick inside of her again.

She still said nothing. Her arms were in a praying position. It just turned Johov on more for another round of fucking.

That's what he did again to her...

...But how could he keep her as a slave? What could he do? He didn't want the other guys to get her. Johov wanted her and no one else.

He had a plan.

...a few hours later, when the bell rang and the soldiers came down to colonize the city, Johov approach another officer in charge.

He grabbed the creature by the neck, like a mother cat does to it's kitten. Cum stained on her body and face. Her hair was abused. She could of died, but she was survived for the exchange of her body. The officer saw Johov approaching him with his bounty.

"Officer! This is my slave! I want her to serve only me! I think she would do fine as an example for others!"

The officer smiled.

"Perfect! Will you be taking her?"

"No. Keep her on this planet we have dominated. I want her branded that I own her. I want to be the only one that can abuse her."

The officer agreed. "Very well then. The creature you have is a fine captive."

Her eyes were closed. She looked directly down. Her figure looked like some kind of cute anime character. As if, she enjoyed being dominated by other foreign men.

...She is still crying and broken inside.

The creature was later identified as M'Khal. She was a nurse for her village. M'Khal was pinched with a microchip to track her entire existence. She was now assigned to a labor camp to do work for the new city for which the Sarparians were building.

Johov left the planet that night. He felt good about himself. He finally had the chance to fuck an alien creature.

…The Midorai are fucking sexy.

He wouldn't mind coming back on the planet and committing a crime to rape one again. He was through with his own Sarparian women. He could care less about helping out the galactic imperium. He could rape wild animals all day.

The next week, he would be off on another planet, trying to kill beast as large as whales. The planet of Mowo was nothing like anything he has ever been on.

He was a "worthy man" now for raping an inferior breed.

…Would he ever see his green bitch again?

Weeks later, Johov would masturbate only to the thought of dominating M'khal. That alien name to... M'khal. Instantly his dick would get hard.

After all this combat, he had to get a new Midorai sex slave! …Or find M'khal again. Yes. Tell her who fucking runs her life!

...And yet, the feeling of a strong guilt would come across his mind.

He actually did rape an animal. How sick was he?

Very sick Johov was.

2.

Xia was born in the year 4040 from the Midorai known as M'khal. She is the bastard daughter of Johov, a Saparian solider. Her birth was a unique once. It was the first instance that the sperm of a Sarparian could pregnant the eggs of a Midorai. M'khal conceived of Xia in three months in the Sarparian month of September. The Midorai monks were surprised that her offspring had a strong resemblance to their Sarparian overlords. The name "Xia" was given her, as it means in ancient tongue, "welcoming." Xia would be a gift to show peace to their new overlords.

For the first seven years of her life, Xia was cared by M'khal. The Midorai had to learn Sarparian speak as their second language. Xia was taught Sarparian speak, along with original Midorai speak, since her education began.

She was quite popular in her elementary school years. She stood out from everyone else. Her white hair was comb to the side like that of an ancient Japanese people. Her animal nose was more pointed, like a Sarparians. And her legs were not zebra-like. She was much smaller than her peers.

194

For the first time, the Midorai had to embrace a mixed-race kind of their own.

But it was in the year 4050, Xia would be sold to a different planet. The Sarparian overlords abused and tortured most of the Midorai. The monk council argued that Xia was a special case, and that she was the daughter of the Sarparians. However, the Imperium frowned upon her as being a bastard and "degenerate" child of mixed-race. The Sarparians would not accept her into the Imperium. Xia did not have blonde hair or blue eyes. She had white hair and slit eyes.

Most female Midorai, the beautiful ones, were sold into prostitution. Xia would be one of them. At the age of 10, the Sarparians sold her to an outpost planet of commerce.

M'khal wished her daughter goodbye, and her gave earrings and a necklace. Earrings once wore by her mother before the Sarparian invasion, and a necklace, featuring the cross of the lord Jaasus. An ancient human deity that once accepted all forms of life, no matter their background or ancestry. Xia, who was both Sarparian and Midorai, would be accepted by a god like Jaasus.

Xia could not understand the things that were going on so young in her life. She dreamed of running away into the wild. Unfortunately, she was oppressed by her new rulers. Now she was being sold somewhere else.

Everything she knew about the past would be distant. At the age of 10, she would begin a new life.

...Xia was handcuffed and was in line for inspection. The alien dealers were the Chauza'has. They were shady creatures in black robes, that looked like prehistoric pterodactyls. They were a sneaky, and exclusives race known for trading. Xia was next in line.

Like an oriental trading market in the Middle-East, One of the Chuza'has inspected Xia with a long stick. The monster smack the stick against her small butt and growing pair of tits.

He looked down upon her. She looked upset.

"This creature, she is different. She should be sold in the sex market immediately. Her mammaries are healthy and exotic. She stands tall and looks submissive. We should sell her for a high price!", said the Chauza'has in his alien tongue.

The other shifty dealers agreed. Xia was moved along into the next room. She was thrown upon a wagon, which would travel to the auction house.

Xia was upset. Strangers would be touching her. She didn't understand what they were saying.

All she wanted was good friends. She wanted to be understood and have a good life.

She felt pain everyday.

Maybe one day, she will be free. The cross of Jaasas reminded her that she was a special person of a greater destiny. Her life was meaningful! It was dark at this moment it time. She had to prevail.

Xia was sold for $100,000 (equivalent to the space currency). She was bought by a mistress named Tschi-Tschi. She herself was of Sarparian blood of aristocratic nobility. Her husband was a CEO of a lucrative resource corporation. She knew how the underground trade worked, for it was operated by decadent upper class elites like herself. Xia was now her little pearl, and Xia's surrogate mom was Ms. T.

She was cruel to Xia. She consider her as an asset to exploit on. The first day when Xia was introduced to Ms. T, she disciplined her to be obedient. Ms. T wore a red phantom mask and had a velvet whip. She never did use her whip. It was use to intimidate those who got out of line.

Ms. T screamed at Xia, "Do what your suppose to do! I am not your mother! You have duties and responsibilities that you must follow! If you do not obey, you will be severely punished!"

Xia understood. Ms. T was not a kind woman at all. She was nothing like her real mother.

Ms. T owned eight other "assets" as she would like to call them. Xia would bond with these other girls. Ms T's inspector, Geinhard Dullard, was to train the girls and give them their duties. Xia was taught to scrub and clean up the mansion for which Ms. T lived in. The decadent and crazy mansion, which was filled every other night with whores and sleazy pimps. Xia had to learn obedience before she could be sold as a call-girl. The other girls Xia was forced to be friends with were far disturbed than her. Three of the girls hated Xia for being a "bitch by birth." Xia never kissed a boy before, nor has ever slept with one.

There was one other girl that Xia could trust. She was also a Midorai. Her name was Sally. An obviously ancient Sarparian sounding name.

Sally was much older than Xia. They quickly became friends. Sally often traumatized Xia before bed every night, with often perverted conversations.

Sally would talk to 10-year-old Xia,

"I suck guy's dicks before. It's nothing special. I actually like the taste of sperm. I get excited when I have to suck a new dick I have never experience before."

Xia in her little naive mind wouldn't understand, "Eww, gross. Why do you have to suck the guy's weaner then?"

Sally would laugh, "Don't you understand how sex works?"

Xia didn't understand the world she was living in. She didn't even understand what "sperm" was either. Sally sounded like some cool kid that has experience so much in the world.

Sally would brag on, "You might not like it at first. I cried the first time I had the guy's junk in my mouth. It was disgusting. I still have trauma from my first time. But it really does go away when it becomes a business. I feel like it was worth it to learn how to please these guys. Most people don't go through what we go through Xia. I take pride in this. I feel I need to suck better dick. I have my own sense of power."

Xia didn't understand what Sally was talking about. Sally, who was only 18, saw the world as a prostitute. Xia would soon be following under her footsteps.

…During the day time, when the girls had to do the chores of Ms. T, they would bicker and fight as they worked. Each girl was of a different race. One girl, by the name of G'hall, belonged to a browner and primitive race known as the Apotoids. The Apotoids were monkey people. Often their societies are crime ridden and self-destructive. G'hall hated Sally because she was always getting "service" on the weekends by wealthy clients. Clients for G'hall was rare. Only the most perverted and weak wanted G'hall's body.

She would curse at Sally.

"Yo you stupid green bitch! Clean the fucking floor faster!"

And Sally would get back at her,

"Mine your fucking own business, you dumb fucking retard!"

Xia would never swear. She didn't understand why the girls would yell each other in such a crude way.

And G'hall continued,

"Clean the fucking floors like how everyone else does then fucking getting it perfect, you dumb Mihik!"

"Mihik," was a stereotype word for a Midorai. The Midorai were known to as submissive perfectionist and collectivist in behavior. Sally felt the pain.

"Fuck you! You piece of shit-skin ape fucker! Your dad fucked a goat!"

Both the girls would bicker on like this.

Xia didn't understand the name calling. She just wanted to get done work and be safe back in her own room. Why did Sally have to be that protective?

…During lunch time, away from the other girls. Xia would ask Sally,

"Why do you call G'hall names?"

"She doesn't care about you are me either. We belong to a different race."

Sally would try her best and explain her racist remarks,

"G'hall is not like me or you. She doesn't care what we do. Xia, you are lucky to be a Midorai. Midorai are the most prettiest and wanted women in the universe. We built an advance society that the Sarparians wished they had made. …You should be lucky to that you have Sarparian blood in yourself as well."

Xia still didn't understand.

"I don't get why you have to be mean to her," Xia said with a naive face.

Sally looked right into her eyes, "See my eyes? They are slanted. Just like yours. G'hall has huge lips and she's fat. We don't have that. We are in the slant eyes club. Ok?"

Xia kind of understood where Sally was coming from.

Sally gave more of her wisdom,

"When you grow up Xia, you are going to be escorting guys of different races and hanging out with your own. The only good race is your own race. Trust someone who is Midorai like yourself. I don't think you are Sarparian, Xia. You are a Midorai. If you ever marry in life, please marry a Midorai. Don't ever marry someone like a Apotoid. Don't even trust a Sarparian, no matter how kind and pleasant he is. Your are going to be a Midorai woman. Be proud of that."

…Gerhard would tell the girls to get back to their positions of work. Lunch would be over.

Xia didn't understand what Sally was talking about. Xia never met her father. And her father is a Sarparian. Why should she be angry against the Sarparian? Jaasus says to give forgiveness for all the sins committed by every alien in the galaxy. Even though she doesn't know her own father, Xia has no hate him. Why should she hate a stranger? She spoke good Sarparian and enjoyed her Midorai culture. She

felt like she didn't belong as fully "Midorai" or "Sarparian."
In her mind, she had a joke she would say to herself when
her teachers would tell she was special. Xia consider
herself as a one-of-a-kind "Maparian." Like the words
"Sarparian" and "Midorai" mixed together. Xia liked being
called a Maparian instead. ...But Sally didn't understand
this quirky humor. Xia was too afraid to tell how she really
felt.

...The girls would work hard and submit to the power of
Ms. T. Xia worked hard for the next two years.

She witnessed awkward events, like coming into a room
when Sally was fucking a stranger, the girls beating each
other to a bloody pulp, not being served food for a full
weeks, and hanging out at an illicit club by herself to get
away from it all.

However, there was one night when Xia felt confusion.

Geinhard Dullard, the man that would command the girls,
was a corrupted and evil man. He was a racial mix of some
sort. He came from an exotic race of some far galaxy, and
had a small bit of Sarparian within him. His dark and alien
appearances was apparent. He dressed and sounded like a
supreme gentlemen, but was a cruel sadist often on power
trips.

One night, when Xia had to work overtime to clean the
dishes for the clients, Geinhard came into the kitchen. Only
those two were in the room together. He said something
like this,

202

"Did you had the chance to have sex yet?"

Xia often would rather focus more on her dish cleaning than talk to him.

"Sex? No, not al all," she would say, like she didn't deserve it.

"Hell, well, I can show you something like it. If you feel like it."

Xia felt like she needed to continue to wash the dishes and ignore him further.

"I don't know Mr. Dullard, wouldn't Ms. T want everything good and tidy, or else I don't get food?," she quickly while still focusing with her work.

Geinhard would touched the back of her hair.

"Nonsense! That woman is a mean person! I will take care of you. What you are doing is amazing and I think you are the best. Ms. T would be proud of you."

Geinhard now grinding against Xia's butt while she has her hands in the sink.

She thought about it,

"You think so? I hope she doesn't yell at me, or ever use that whip against me. I don't like that."

"She won't babe. You have an nice body. ...Let's have sex right now! It's really easy. I can show you."

Geinhard's hand was feeling up Xia's small and growing breast. She didn't know what to do. Geinhard, a much older man, was feeling up a little girl. Is this okay?

"I don't know. I really don't know what I am suppose to do right, ...now," She said as she putt the dishes away."

Geinhard smiled.

"You have such nice hair. Please, let me kiss you."

Geinhard went up to Xia to give her a kiss. She liked the kissed. It wasn't so bad. She smiled back at him.

"Oh well, Mr. Dullard, I didn't know you wanted to do it now... and, well, that's nice of you, and...", She said in confusion.

"Nobody knows we are in here. Let's just have sex right now!", he said.

Geinhard took his arms around Xia's waist and started to move into Xia's mouth.

"Oh boy, I'm not sure if I am suppose to do this boss," she said with even more confusion.

The emotions were overwhelming. She was once working, now all of a sudden, she's kissing the strict boss. It felt so soft and warm. What was going on? His tongue entered into her mouth. She didn't even know how to kiss. His arm was grabbing her small tit. It felt so warm like he loved her. ...Did Geinhard love her? That's was the thought racing in her head. Is this love? She felt all the spit around her mouth.

"Sir, umm, this is nice. It's funny your doing this to me. I don't know what to say..." she would say as an incoherent statement.

Geinhard hard his left hand spreading out Xia's white hair and had his right hand unzipping his pants.

"Alright, if your going to be a good girl, your going to have to show it."

He pulled down his pants. Something hard was in his underwear. He took it out, and his hard penis was getting bigger. This was the first time Xia was approached with a penis. The thing that Sally always talked about, "penises."

Geinhard's penis was moldy. His testicles were huge. His penis was the size of Xia's cheeks. It was growing. He flipped out the dick with his fingers to make it extend. Xia smiled for a bit.

"Oh, that thing. Umm, wow." She said (she really didn't know what to say). She didn't know how to react. She laughed.

Geinhard's smile grew. She put Xia down on her knee and moved his penis into her face.

"Like it? All good girls know how to suck a dick. It's what they deserve when they wash the dishes and be good. You deserve this cock," he said to her.

It was erecting. She was being pushed into the wall. She could not go away. At first, she dodge her head to the ground, neglecting it was there. It was either the penis or the floor. Geinhard had a solid stomach like a stone wall. Xia grab the penis with her hands. She jerked it up and down. She never put a guy's thing in her mouth before. Not only did she get her first kiss by a guy right now, she's also getting her first cock in her mouth. Geinahrd was rubbing his dick against her cheeks. Xia was giggling. He was so tall, and she was so short. Xia kissed the penis forehead with her lips. She did it a couple of times before putting it in her mouth. Her eyes closed. He tongue was on it. She didn't know any motion on how to suck a dick or any techniques Sally taught her (she wasn't listening). ...It was too big for her. Gernhard had both his hands on her hair. Xia was worried whatever it was okay to suck the inspector's dick or not. She was being reward for her good job, right?

...After the event, Xia came back to Sally's Bedroom. Sally was bored, looking at the ceiling and doing nothing. Xia was anxious and nervous. Sally could tell something was up.

"What's wrong?"

Xia sat on the other side of Sally's bed.

"Well umm, actually, for the first time, umm, I did it."

"You did what?"

"Well, umm, I, sucked a guy's dick," she said in a quiet tone.

She said it as if it was an embarrassing secret. Though at the same time, she felt it was some kind of "rite of passage" towards adulthood. She felt some inner pride that she sucked a guy's dick.

Sally was amused.

"Really? No way."

Xia was shaking a little. She said, "Yeah really! He like, shot sperm on my face", as she waved on her cheek to show Sally. Xia felt the cold, dry and white cum stain on her face. There was dried up sperm flakes of Geinhard's in Xia's white hair.

Sally looked over Xia's face. She noticed the flake.

"Really? Get out!" Sally now interested like a a high school girl who found out about a crushes secret.

"It's in your hair! Haha, who was the guy? Tell me! What did you do, what happened?"

Xia felt a little better about the situation. Even though it was extremely awkward, Sally told it like it was Xia's first time kissing a guy. Xia thought that maybe Sally was taking this thin too seriously. Maybe it was a really good experience, and she didn't know why.

"Umm, well, yeah, it was awesome. I liked it," Xia said to Sally.

"I can tell your a little startled. Seriously though, your not at all mad or anything?" Sally had a surprised tone in her voice.

Xia looked down at her feet. How big Geinhard was. She had to tell Sally it was good anyway.

"Yeah. It was pretty good. I liked it," Xia said with a smile.

3.

   Johov was alone. He had no one to go to. He always went to the bar by himself to get drunk every other night.

The Terminal Bar was infamous for it's seedy culture.

His duty for the Imperium was over. There was no motivation to get a good paying job. It was better to live on welfare.

Trauma haunted Johov.

...How long has it been since he raped an alien? He can't remember.

Johov sat alone in the bar with a beer in his hand. Another loud and crowded night. There was nothing to do.

The bartender knew who he was. A Sarparian who has seen the galaxy, but came back as an unproductive citizen.

Johov had thoughts of suicide. But he was too cowardly to do it.

The TVs blared tons of incoherent messages.

"Prime York Odins vs the Liberty City Orcs."

"Tonight! Boring Reality TV Show!"

"News of another Islamic bombing!"

What do any of these subliminal messages mean? Another commercial to swindle your money. No one ever trusted the media.

Reckless Sarparians and aliens hanged out at the Terminal.

—The lower class types.

Johov had no parents. He had no honest upbringing. He was a product for a material upper-class. A bio-engineered solider to fight for their wars. Johov was never rewarded for his duty.

Another sip.

Everything was loud and distorted. Inside Johov's mind, was silence. A single trauma raced through his head over and over again.

"Hey!"

An Apotoid or some Seeger breed approached Johov.

"What's up big man? Having fun?"

Johov wasn't having fun. He wanted to be left alone. The feminine creature sat right next to him. Johov noticed her bouncy ass.

She noticed.

"Want to do something fun? Wanna fuck? It's all on you!"

Great. Another hooker.

Johov use to have fun with them. Now it's annoying. She's asking for money. Might as will give her some cash and let her shut the fuck up.

...Or why not hate-fuck her? Fuck and abuse her? She's annoying to begin with.

Her ass is pretty good. Not even from a good breed either. Seegers are working class whores, so foreign and unfit for the Sarparians, the supreme gentlemen of the galaxy.

Why not rape her and show her who's boss?

Johov chatted with the begging slut. Her name was S'wha.

"S'wha." What a cheesy porn star name.

Johov agreed on her terms. However, he wanted to fuck right now in the bathroom. And if he brutally hurts her enough, she won't be asking for any money and he walk away with a free fuck.

Dirty sex with the clothes on.

The motion was so good. But Johov wanted her feeling pain. He went much faster. Her ass smacking against Johov's pants.

"Ahhh, ooohhh, fuck," she said.

"Fucking little bitch!" Johov yelled at her. The dance music made the scene more of an ecstasy.

Johov smacked S'wha on the ground. She was his bitch to abuse.

Then at that moment, something happened. The angry, nihilistic Johov had a change of heart.

As he was raping his exploited meat, he noticed the motion of S'wha's Apotoid-like ass. Furry, brown, large, and moldy like. The way it moved up and down on his cock. Like jelly. The ass was very warm for an aggressive indirect "saleswoman" like her. This fucking transaction reminded Johov of a certain someone a decade ago.

Back on Mowo.

His duty as a soldier for the Imperium.

His giant barbaric space suit.

Him raping a Midorai.

That was the best fuck he ever had in his life. That was his first fuck and his best. He never did rape another alien after that. He never told another a Sarparian that he raped an animal, fearing that he would be made fun of. When he got back to Terra, hookers were fun and exciting. Now realizing, looking at S'wha, how fucking digesting she was.

...But her ass. Like a mother's ass. A sweet kind ass that is caring and loving. That was S'wha's ass. Her ass was just like that Midorai he fucked long ago.

...What was that Midorai name? ...M'khal! M'khal is one and only true love!

Johov came inside of S'wha.

After taking out his cock, he pushed down S'wha on the ground. A long cum-string reached from his cock to her ass. She was highly overwhelmed with Johov's abuse. She couldn't get up. Johov quickly got up, tuck in his pants, and immediately left the bar. S'wha was beaten and left for dead. After the loud noises and when her post-organism finally goes away, she could get up and take her daily abortion pills. ...and take Johov's money?

Johov left the Terminal. He was racing back to his apartment like he forgot something. He was running away from the the scene of the crime. Johov had a revelation.

He had to go home right now and find out where M'khal is.

...M'khal, the name he learned about a week after he fucked her.

Did she ever had a kid? Is she married? What doe she do? Can she understand Sarparian speak? Does she like walks in the parks, flowers and rainbows?

Johov was going mad. His life was utterly meaningless without her. He finally understood why he was so depressed.

He is a violent monster, yes. But he can undue his sins once he can be with M'khal again. His true sex slave.

Johov remember old documents he left in his closet. Looking over it, he realized he had a serial code for her.

Name: M'khal
Code: 667844859934830

The cute picture of her. She looked so sad. Like if she had to pose for a picture at gunpoint... which was probably true.

If Johov entered this code into the Imperium slave database, he could find where she is and claim her as his sex slave.

...Even better, make her his loving wife. His wife that will learn Sarparian speak, that will cook for him, that will sleep with him, and that will always call him when he's away...

Everything he ever wanted in life. True love. They can both live on welfare, until they both find shitty jobs as cashier's somewhere in the mega city. Something like that.

No more going to the bar. This is it. Johov was going to find out where she was.

He spent hours on virtual internet. He was looking up the history of the Midorai, finding information on M'khal, and learning about the Midoria culture. Where he could buy a teleporter to Mohawii? It was going to be expensive.

…Who cares? He will be living like a vegabond once he gets to Mowo. He is of Sarparian blood. He should be the new ruler once her gets on the new planet!

…The culture of the Midorai was so interesting. It was better than his own Sarparian culture he knew of. The Midorai preached love for centuries until the Sarparians invaded their planet ten years ago. The Midorai also invented their own system of writing, of architect, of music, of literature, of visual arts…

…Midorai life was so different than living in the crowded city ruled by the Sarparians.

The Midorai don't have cities! They live in small trusted communities and everyone knows each other! Wow.

Johov felt a deep sense of belonging. And a thought came across his mind, "Why haven't I experience such a good life?"

Suddenly, depression came kicking back in.

Johov couldn't just leave his poverty and escape towards adventure. No way. What was he thinking? Where is he going? M'khal is most likely dead by now. She is suffering in her own existence somewhere else. Why would Johov want to find her? Why would she want to be friends with her rapist?

...No. It wasn't about rape. It was more than that. This was his destiny.

Johov was running away from his destiny for ten years. M'khal was his wife to be!

Johov is an animal fucker. He has to embrace his inner-self as a freak.

...Then again... he cant. There is no such thing as a Sarparian wedding a Midorai. ...Can they even have kids?

Depression sank into Johov.

Johov laid alone in his bed. He turned out the lights.

Four hours into the night, researching about the Midorai race and M'khal's existence. ...It was useless.

It was an excuse. He would be back in that bar raping girls and thinking about M'khal. He should not step foot in the Terminal bar again, or else S'wha's pimp is going to kill him.

There is a bigger meaning to life than fucking a stranger.

Fucking creates children. Children are the future. ...Johov fucked M'khal. He should take as a responsibility.

...Her beautiful ass. That curvy, nice, healthy virgin alien ass he fucked. His dick felt so soft inside of her. It felt so warm. She liked it too. M'khal was blessed with such a giant foreign cock like Johov's. It felt so good.

...S'wha ass was disgusting...

...But the nostalgia of his first ass! The ass that could never be replaced.

Johov had to fuck that Midorai ass again.

He masturbated in bed alone. His sperm shot all the way to his neck.

Shooting inside of S'wha was an unexciting flood of sperm.

Jerking off to his first love, was like a natural fountain. His cock at it's best.

Alone in his bed Johov laid. Sad.

Ejaculating felt like he pulled the trigger against himself.

Sperm laid on his body. The stuff that could be his future children. He was defeated.

Headache, tired, sad. Johov might as well sleep all day tomorrow. There was no reason to fight.

Shirtless, pants down, looking at the alarm clock.

5AM.

What a night. A sudden change of events. Four hours doing research on nothing.

Could he ever go and find out where his true love is? Where is she?

Johov's life never made sense. All he ever wanted was to live a good life.

This decadent Sarparian life is garbage. …Lies about a supreme race, to murder and conquer innocent people, and an act in a certain, uptight way.

This was not Johov. He is a byproduct of his twisted society. There was no reason to argue for the truths of the Imperium.

The Midorai and their wisdom have a better culture and people. They lived in peace. The Imperium invades and destroys.

Johov wanted to change his life around. No longer was he going to be a depressed Sarparian solider. …He was going to be an expert on Midorai culture.

He was going to find and marry M'khal.

…Rolling around in his bed. Sad. Could he ever find where she is? Or is he doomed forever?

Johov went to sleep in his bed. Alone.

4.

Years later, Xia experienced the routines of demanding promiscuous sex and mundane work. She was the perfect little girl to do the dishes and suck cock.

There were exciting times when she got one inside of her. The first time it was awkward, and again, it was with Geinhard Dullard. One client was extremely good at it and she enjoyed sex for the first time. That was a year ago. She is now 17-years-old.

Xia and Sally remained close friends. Last night for the first time, she and Sally had their first gang bang together. It was awkward seeing Sally naked on top of another stranger. It was also weird to suck a cock with Sally sucked the testicles. Together with an older girl like Sally, It made Xia even more attractive. Her charming naivety and shyness made her beautiful. Everyone wanted to put a dick in Xia's mouth. The way her droopy eyes looked so sad looking at the clients. Her mouth, which drooled all over the cock, while her head went up and down on it. She was a young princess everyone wanted.

However, she was getting bored of sex. Sally learn to love the sport. Xia thought it was something disgusting she had to do to survive another day.

The next day, Xia had a sleazy client of an unknown species. The guy wanted his dick sucked along with a titty-fuck. Xia hated titty-fucking. Her tits were finally growing this year. She had two plump peach tits. Easy to grab with both hands. Hard as rocks.

This reptilian client had a hard and scaly cock that was like a mace. Green, uncircumcised, and lizard-like. His sperm oozed purple!

Xia was so annoyed at his perverted nature, he let him use his own hands to titty-fuck himself. There sat Xia on her knees with a bored face, as the reptile man used his hands stretching Xia's tits up and down on his lizard cock. Xia's tit jiggled like drips in a water. She felt the pain.

"Oh shit! Oh yeah, yeah you little bitch! You like that shit?"

Xia didn't even laugh. This guy was lewd and disgusting. He should pop and get it over with.

His purple sperm oozed out like water balloon popping. It wasn't pissy or sticky like white Sarparian sperm, with was like puddy and gooey.

"Eat that shit bitch!", he insisted.

Xia really didn't want to. She closed her eyes as she licked the fluid substance. The reptile was getting high off her supposed pain.

Luckily, Xia didn't swallow any of his alien sperm. The client was quite please and took photos of her. She didn't want to smile. She made a face as if the guy did something wrong. The guy loved it and thought it was some kind of secret admiration. The reality was, she was really mad at him.

As she got up, the lizard grouped her ass and flexed it a couple of times. Topless, drenched in purple reptilian sperm and wearing sexy pink yoga pants. Great.

Xia finally had the chance to wash up in the bathroom. She looked at herself in the mirror. She had a headache last night with that gang bang, and now she's covered in purple shit. She didn't want to work today at all.

There at the door, Sally stood there. She laughed at Xia's nudity.

"Oh my god! What the fuck happen to you, girl? Let me help clean you! …Where are you getting fucked up again?"

"Please. I didn't like it at all. It's fucking embarrassing," Xia said to Sally.

"No shit! You look like you were having fun in a mud pit or something."

Sally grabbed a cloth and started rubbing off the purple globs of sperm off Xia's green skin.

"I have a total headache and don't want to go through this. Tell Ms. T I'm absent for the rest of the day. I'm pissed off."

Sally had a curious plan to share with Xia. She didn't want to tell it to her last night. Sally was caught in the moment enjoying the good fuck. Xia obviously didn't like it, and her mood was not good.

"Hey, yo, you don't have to tell that fat bitch Ms. T anything. I wanted to tell you something."

"Tell me what?"

Sally threw the purple towel into the trash.

"We don't have to work here anymore!"

"What do you mean?", Xia said while she was getting the sperm off her eyelids.

"So, I was talking to Hashi last night. You know, the other Midorai girl? And she offered me and you to run away from this place."

Xia was surprised. "Runaway? You mean like, leave our rooms?"

"Hell yeah. Do you remember we had the privilege to roam the cities outside the mansion? It was fun right?"

"Totally..." Xia thought about it for a second.

"And like, Ms T doesn't even fucking need us anymore. And we don't fucking need her. We can leave whenever we want and be our own free girls. She's just some fat whore that makes money off of us. Hashi has a place we can crash at with her."

Xia liked the sound of that.

"Wait, hold on. Well, what about the other girls? Don't they care if we leave them without notice?"

"Fuck them. That one fucking twat Twaci left without notice. No one gives a shit anymore Xia. Your that age too! I use to be a runaway all the time when you first came here too. But I stayed because, I don't know, I love you."

Xia heard the words "I love you." The special words she always wanted to hear.

"Really? I like you too Sally."

Sally put her arms around Xia's shoulders while looking in the mirror. Dried purple sperm laid on Xia's chest.

"You and I are like sisters. I fucking love you! I know your going to find a good man in your life. Not some dumb fucking turtle fucker who jerks off on you."

Xia liked what she said. She had a mental connection to Geinhard Dullard. Dulluard left two years ago. That was the past. She should move on to find a new man.

And Sally told her she was raped and that she wanted move on from the trauma. Xia wished she could do something more in her life than fuck strangers. She had the ambitious to become a nurse just like her forgotten mother.

"You think I could work as a nurse? Do I have to go to school for that?"

"Fuck yeah baby! You can do that! All you have to do is approach them and say you want it!"

Xia laughed and smiled.

"Come one Xia. Let's fucking get out of here. Let's leave tonight! Hashi is on her way. We are fucking leaving this place for good. Don't tell anyone."

…Sally had to get her tampons and leave the room.

Xia liked what she was hearing. Was this for real? Was she going to run away with her best friend Sally and start a new life out in the city of Mohawii? Does she finally have the choice to become an adult?

As Xia put on a shirt, she looked at herself in the mirror again.

White hair, big cheeks, cute eyes, nice green skin with a pushed-in, dog-like nose. Guys wanted Xia. It didn't matter if she was raped by a stranger every other day. She could start a new life.

...Maybe she could be a mother and finally raise kids!

Tonight was the night she would leave this place for good.

...And that's exactly what she did.

Right before bed, she and Sally caught Hashi's car. She didn't tell Ms. T or anyone that they were leaving.

As Hashi drove up, she looked back at the mansion she spent the last seven years in. Good memories and strange pains. All now apart of the past.

…The girls got to their new location at a lonely apartment. Hashi use to share the space with her then arrogant boyfriend. He left. Now it was just them together.

Each girl had their own room to sleep in. For the first time, Xia had a sense of privacy. She took her first hot shower in ages. She was so happy to be alive.

To celebrate their freedom, Hashi had something in mine.

"Hey, there is this one cute guy at this tattoo parlor and I was thinking of getting something on my back. Would any of you like a free tattoo?"

Sally had to call Xia in her room.

"Xia! Do you want to go out and get a tattoo?"

"What's that?"

"A tattoo? You should totally get one!"

Xia came down stairs in a single white shirt and shorts.

"What's going on?", she said.

"You want to get a tattoo, Xia? You should get one at your age."

Xia thought about it. …A tattoo? Why would she need one?

"Are you getting one?"

"Sure, I need one on my left thigh. I already have this guy on the other side."

Xia forgot Sally had at least one tattoo in the past.

The tattoo design was of an oriental Sarparian woman, with a large "yakuza" back print and fire all around her. It suited Sally's personify. Sally always wanted to be part of some royal Sarparian blood, even though she was not and often she would tell Xia how much she really hated Sarparians.

The tattoo did intrigue Xia. She wanted to do something tonight.

She said, "Sure, lets go."

"Awesome!"

…Off they went to the tattoo parlor.

Tattoos have always remained special within centuries of living beings. Originally worn by the Sarparians, aliens around the galaxy now don tattoos. From the mentally disturbed, the upper-class hipsters, and the criminal-minded.

Xia, Sally and Hashi all belong to an oppressed group of minorities known as the Midorai.

Hashi had sleeves of tattoos on her. Some of them ranged from classical Sarparian-Russian tattoos to quirky low-brow cartoons. However, she was conservative in attitude. Once she was a sex slave like Xia and Sally, now she is her own free woman. She works as a waitress for a multi-alien sports bar. Though her dream has always been to marry a man from a higher class and take her as his wife. Hashi was flirting with a Sarparian tattoo artist she met at work. He was a nice guy and would offer free tattoos for her recently acquired girlfriends.

"Xia, we should get matching tattoos! Like sister to sister!", Sally said to her.

Xia was scrolling through a book of possible tattoos she could get. All of them were scary and evil. That wasn't her style.

"I don't know. All of these marks don't describe me."

"Who the fuck cares if they don't 'describe' you. You get whatever you fucking want and you keep getting more to show your friends," Sally said with pride.

Xia was reconsidering getting a tattoo now. Before Sally got on the bench to get a random tattoo, she thought about something long ago.

…Xia had a memory of her mother that would show her a picture book of the world. The first people to discover Mowo were the gentle Asian-Aryan people. The Asian-Aryan people introduced old-human-Sarparian-Asian culture to the Midorai. Xia's mother would tell her that the Midorai are spiritual beings descended from a great race know as the Orientals. The Orientals ranged from a selected group of Sarparian beings that were the first to create galactic civilization. The Orientals wore pretty dresses and fought against giant creatures known as "dragons." Xia remembered her mom telling her that the Midorai were descended from these dragons.

Xia had a fascination not only with Sarparian English, but as well with the ancient script of the human-Chinese language. She remembered a script of Chinese she discovered in a childhood picture book that meant "love, family, and rebirth." She would draw this symbol all the time in her coloring books.

Xia needed to have that symbol on her.

She asked the parlor man, "Excuse me, but do you have anything with Chinese art?"

"Over there," he pointed.

A huge brown book that was filled with ancient symbols. Xia was amazed with the art in this book. Not anything scary, angry or evil art. It was blissfully good.

Then all off a sudden, she found the exact same script, along with other nostalgic scripts she remembered.

Love, Family and Rebirth.

She had to get a tattoo now.

Xia sat herself on the table like a giddy girl waiting for a lollypop.

"What do you want?" the guy said.

"This, right here," she pointed in the book.

"I want it... I want it here!", she pointed to the side of her belly. ...But don't make it too big! The same size in the book!"

"...Are you sure you don't want it on your arm?," he said.

Sally was already waiting for some paint to get on her skin.

"Fucking get two Xia. Do it."

She thought about it.

"No, here is fine."

"Whatever the lady wants," he said.

...A few hours later, Xia was in the backroom checking out her tat. She could not touch or disturb it. It hurt a bit, but the results were worth it. She was holding out her stomach. Xia felt somewhat ashamed that she was eating too much recently out of anxiety. She had a little belly gut. There was the tattoo. Her weight wasn't that bad. All she has to do was to eat less and hit the treadmill when she had the chance.

Sally walked in.

"Let me see your new tat!"

Xia showed her gut instead. The tattoo was above it.

"You think I'm fat?" she said to Sally.

Sally didn't notice.

"Super cute Xia. I like it. What is it?"

Xia was surprised.

"You don't know what it is?"

"No what is it?"

"It's written in Chinese. It's like, our old ancestors. It means Love, Family, Rebirth."

"I totally see that with you. We are family," Sally said with a smile.

Sally showed the tattoo under her wrist.

"Check this out."

Her tattoo displayed a Buddha-like messiah on a nailed cross. The design was so esoteric, Sally did not know of it's original origin.

"Hold on, fuck. Let's take a selfie together."

Sally had an advance media app that would take a picture of both her and Xia together. Sally would hold Xia by her side like if she was her sister. Xia felt a little embarrassed since the camera was pointing at her flabby skin. Sally didn't seem to care.

"Shit. Let me go get Hashi and show you her tats."

Xia looked at herself in the mirror one last time. She was a growing up to be a good young woman. Even if she had a growing gut, she still liked the way she looked. That tattoo made her even more prettier. She did a couple of poses looking herself in the mirror.

Everything she knew in the past was an old trauma. She could start a whole new life again as new woman. She was a special person, from both a Sarparian and Midorai mix blood.

Xia was finally starting to love her life.

5.

     Angry. Alone. Life was becoming more depressing for Johov. There was nothing left in life. He could not afford his ticket to Mowo, the birth of his happiness. He was in debt.

Looking at the ceiling. Death was contemplating him.

Walks didn't work anymore either. He would be passing by the same scum of society. Everything was so multicultural and decadent. The Imperium sold out it's home planet to foreign aliens. From Apotoids, Seegers, Gillatoko, whatever takes a shit in the street. There was no such thing as a Midorai on Terra.

Johov's happiness was stripped. All these alien types made society worse. They were all begging for the pie that the Sarparians had created. Hypocrites. None of these aliens really strived off Sarparian culture. The Sarparians used all the aliens they captured and made them little pets to groom and show the galaxy they dominated over them. ...so much for the Imperium.

Why would the Sarparians be beneficial for this galaxy anyway? Terra should be for the Sarparians only.

...Liars. This whole life is a lie.

...Johov was going to start a new revolution. He owned some nuclear mini-bombs used in combat.

This was it.

Johov would walk back in that stupid bar he always hated, press the button, and kill himself. Blow himself up with that bomb-strap. Johov wanted to go out gracefully in this pathetic life.

According to Midorai culture, killing oneself retained the honor of the individual.

Johov wasn't another Sarparian slave. He was an "enlightened" Sarparian, liberating the Midorai from their colonial oppression.

The Midorai must be free from the Imperium.

This was Johov's final day.

He walked outside his apartment, looked both ways, and continued down the street.

The seething mass of useless aliens. Worthless. All would grow up and die. All had meaningless lives.

Johov was the only Sarparian walking the streets. A true Sarparian belonged to a aristocratic order. There was no such thing as a "poor" Sarparian. But Johov was one of the "wrong kind" of Sarparians.

How the Sarparians had lied to him! Sarparians are the most inauthentic people in the existence of the known galaxy! The women are tardy, the men are barbaric... who cares if they invented "civilization?" To take pride being a Sarparian means idiocracy. There is no progress with this race!

A loud noise came from the center of the street. Some kind of band was playing electronic music.

This was it. He could let go of the bomb here and blow up everyone.

...Maybe. Some stupid teen idol was playing to make the bastard aliens feel good about life.

Fuck that kid.

Johov kept moving on.

The loud noise of the city was irritating. Society never loved the loner. He felt out of place every step he made walking alone.

Should he just go home and cry himself like he always does?

No. It's going to take another painful year to clear his debt, and another two years to afford to get out of this place.

Today was the day. This was it.

There was the Terminal bar. No one goes in the day time. Should he let himself go without a warning and blow himself up in front of the bar? …Agian, it was a maybe.

Johov looked up at the vintage neon sign of the bar. One of the only neon signs left on the planet. Should he walk in?

…Then something happened.

A woman passed by Johov with two shady men. The girl had green skin.

…Was it her?

They shuffled passed Johov. He look at their backs. The girl looked sad.

…Was it a Midorai?

Johov followed the gang behind them. He had nothing to lose.

The girl was weeping.

"Shut up you!", the guy said.

The gang walked behind an ally way. Johov turned towards the direction.

Suddenly, one of the men pulled out a knife on the girl.

He said, "Listen you fucker. If you don't pay us now, your going to get beat!"

The girl was mewling like an animal.

White hair. …She was a Midorai. One of a kind.

Johov had to intervene.

"Stop!" he said. "What are you doing to her!?"

All three looked back at the stressed Johov that followed them in a back alley.

"Who the fuck are you?", the guy said.

"Leave her alone!", Johov said back.

Both men pulled out their knifes. These were thugs that didn't want anyone ratting out on their criminal deeds.

Johov could detonate the strap now.

…He didn't want to. He was ready to get stabbed to death.

A fight broke out. Johov took some punches, and then punched one back in the face. Throwing, kicking, stomping, and smacking. Johov was able to take on the two.

The girl huddled on the ground as she watched.

Johov knocked out one guy. The other guy sliced Johov's arm. Johov kicked him on the ground.

…Both men finally ran away.

The girl then was looking straight at Johov. He went up to her.

She was a Midorai. It reminded him of someone else in his life.

"You ok?", he said, bloodied and bruised.

The girl got up and ran away from him.

"Where are you going?", he said.

The girl was back on the street again. This time, a Sarparian with blonde hair and handsome appeal showed up. The girl hugged him in his arms.

Johov saw them. ...A Sarparian? When did anyone come down from the great towers?

This Sarparian was holding the Midroai girl in his arms, like *he* saved her.

The Midorai pointed back at Johov.

"That man! He's trying to kill me! He beat up Sogo's men and now he wants to kill me!"

...No, this is a misunderstanding!

The Sarparian man said, "Him? That guy?"

"Yes! He's up to no good!"

"I will call the cops on him!"

Johov didn't understand what was going on. He saved the Midorai girl's life, and now his... Sarparian boyfriend is calling the cops on him!?

"Stay away from my girl!", the Sarparian man said while coming towards Johov. He was ready for a fight.

How was this happening? The Midorai girl that Johov was protecting, was now against him? And she has a cocky Sarparian boyfriend?

Why isn't it him? Johov should be her boyfriend!

The Sarparian pushed Johov onto the ground.

Angry, upset, he had to let himself go.

Johov reached down, and pressed the button.

...Everyone died.

6.

Xia was a young adult now. 24 years old. She had lots of experience since her freedom from Ms. T. Sally and Hashi became her best friends. Xia for about three years had a good Sarparian-mixed boyfriend. She recently left him because he had annoying habits.

Xia was free to do what she wanted to do.

She was a bartender for a club outside her apartment. Xia loved talking to strangers and getting involved with the petty drama of the lower classes. Xia felt that her Midorai identity was special. The Midroai sticked around each other and kept their affairs secret.

Xia felt liberated when it came to the Sarparian men and mixes that would approach her. Sally and Hashi would have their many devoted Midorai boyfriends. The Midorai men were quite feminine and "asian" looking. Both the sexes had two totally two different personalities. ...How could the Midorai reproduce with two sexes that conflict with each other? Sally and Hashi have been with their boyfriends for the past five years. Xia was the one that flirted and dated many different guys. She realized that she was always after a different type of Sarparian guy.

Xia had a thing for them. Sarparian men were the best. They seem to have the traits of a gentlemen, but the aggressive nature of a barbarian. Midorai women were weak and submissive. A Sarparian man and his Midorai girl were a perfect match together.

Xia offered sex service exclusively to Sarparian guys. She had an offer tonight from a wealthy looking and thrill seeking Sarparian man by the name of Mark.

Xia offered titty-fucking service for a large amount of Imperium credits.

Xia loved sex, but it was not her identity. She knew had to use sex as a tool. Sally and Hashi always told her that she had a nice pair of peach-titties that every guy wanted to grope and suck. Sally and Hashi's tits were quite normal. Xia had the small body, but with the perfect, round and fat, water-balloon boobs. Whenever Xia would tuck herself in her small jeans, her tits would shake.

Xia's previous Sarparian boyfriend was good at fucking. She eventually learned about the dichotomy between good and bad sex. She became a master at the game. Though she would not call herself an "alpha," but rather a call-girl on demand for the needy, beta Sarparian boys she would love to jerk. Every Sarparian consumer Xia had was a dream boy.

Casually, she would call the guy to the back of the bar, where she would take off her shirt, and would start tittyfucking on her knees. She trusted Sarparians enough to play with her white hair and body. For an extra charge, she would kiss the dick or suck it. That was the best time to catch a guy in the moment, where she could milk them for extra cash.

Mark had a nice 7-inch-dick. He wore boxers. A big guy. The two didn't seem to fit well with each other (in a cute way). His dick was sliding through Xia's balloon tits like sandpaper. It was a little painful.

Xia loved to laugh at the awkward moments. (One time she put on perfume before a customer, and then the dick she sucked tasted like the perfume odor she put on. It was her fault).

Xia's tits always jiggled like jelly when guys shook her tits with their soft cocks. Xia loved that feeling.

Some guy's dicks exploded at times when she least expected it. Xia believed that Sarparian sperm had beauty power to it. Sarparian sperm had a nice sticky feeling to it, between water and milk. It cleaned acme when it reached the skin. Some of said the best way to have a clean face is to rub Sarparian sperm in the face. Any other alien sperm was exotic and strange for Xia. Sarparian sperm was white. White, and natural, healthy and good color to have on the skin.

Mark's dick popped on Xia's tits. Some splashes of sperm fell on her chin, and the rest as a puddle on her titties. Like a race horse, Xia calmed down the Sarparian dick by stroking it a bit and kissing it.

"Good boy, calm down!", she would jokingly say with her Sarparian clients. Jerking them off was like cuddling with a cute animal.

All the Sarparian men wanted her. Xia liked every single Sarparian guy she was ever with. She considered them all her brothers.

Xia loved it when the guys said how beautiful she was or even how "messy" she was (she liked when they talked dirty). But she hated it when guys treated her like shit (and Sarparian men were never like that).

She also loved the random nature of Sarparians. Some of the guys would slap her ass and call her cute names. Xia loved it when guys would ask for her future contacts. She was always happy to make new friends and keep steady relationships with her Sarparian clients.

However, Xia was at a point in her life where she wanted to quit sex-for-money and become a mother of three kids.

Mark looked like a good candidate to be her husband. Even though he wasn't skilled in anything, he had a kind heart and showed devotion starting a family.

…But like in every family, the two had to make a vow not to sleep with anyone else. Xia had to trust Mark he if was going to do the same.

After the expensive titfucking, she would clean up and work the bar until 5AM. Her friends Sally and Hashi were nocturnal creatures too.

Sally was much older than Xia. Her boyfriend was soon going to propose to her.

"Hi Xia! How was Mark? Did you fuck again?", Sally said with a laugh.

"I mean, he just jerked of on my tits like always. Same old."

"Do you like him?", Sally said to her like a big sister.

Xia smiled, "Yeah, I do. He's a nice guy. I think he has everything under control. We are still snapping each other and it looks like he's seeing other girls at the moment."

"Watch out. He could change his mind any second. I have been with Tony for about five years Xia… You know he… proposed to me?"

Xia didn't believe what Sally was saying. "Get out. Really?"

"Hell yeah! Tony is totally clean. He's not lying or making up shit like he does. He seriously wants to move out to the suburbs and start a family. He's got this new job as a construction worker and he told me he's okay marrying someone who is of a different race!"

"Wow! Really? Did he say that?"

"Yes! It's true! He's so open about it! It like, never happens… but it shows you, Tony is open about it and he is an honest and caring person! …So are you going to get with Mark?"

Xia started laughing, "Oh gee! I don't know, should I?"

"Girl, you been fucking him for the last six months and he would totally want to wife you up. Your such a cute girl, anyone would want you."

Xia started to blush.

"Are you sure you want to be with Tony? Tony is Sarparian. I thought you were into Ackold or, you know…"

"No, no, no. I ditched him. He's a good guy and all. He's nothing like Tony. …Xia, your right about something. I remember I told you a long time ago to stick with people of your own race, do you remember that?"

"…I'm not sure."

"Well, I learned something from you Xia. It's okay to be with people of your own race. But, what I am learning as I get older, there are some guys outside our own race that can totally benefit our lives! I mean, I love Tony! I never thought a Sarparian guy would take care of me and tell me how much I am his princess! I really like Sarparian now. They are like, a match made in heaven with Midorai girls."

"Really!?", Xia said with excitement.

"Totally! Shit, at first, I thought you were a little crazy slut with a nice pair of tits that went after Sarparian guys only for the attention. Now like, your working the guys and telling everyone who's boss. I totally admire you for that, Xia."

"Thank you", Xia said. She never heard such kind words from Sally before. Xia would always be looking up to Sally and Hashi for wisdom, but now, Sally was learning something from Xia.

"I always liked Sarparian culture. I learned Sarparian-English at a young age, and I always wanted to know about their civilization. I took pride that I was half-Sarparian. I thought I also had an advantage because I was mixed too. I still feel that… and, you know…"

"You don't have to tell me. Sarparian cock is the best, right?"

Both of the girls started laughing.

"No! There is nothing wrong being Midorai! I think that Midorai girls are better off with Sarparian guys, and both cultures enriching us… and…"

"I know how you feel. Like, I love being Midroai. But, I love to be a Midorai *with* a Sarparian boyfriend! It's totally awesome."

"…But think about the children you are going to have to…"

"Yes, a bunch of little Xias! How adorable!"

Both the girls were having fun laughing about the thought of their futures.

Eventually, Xia had to cut short the conversation and get back to work. She and Sally would talk later. Things were looking good.

…Being a hot and wanted alien girl was amazing. Xia's life, which was once brutal and abusive, was now turning around and becoming clean and orderly. Even though she had to hang around the sleazy underground culture, and do her whore gig (which she is not ashamed of), Xia was planning for the day to become a mother. She wanted her children to live a better life than what she went through.

She could of died in the underground. Although, she has learned to take pride being a sexy, tattooed Midorai girl of the sleazy underground. It was a matter of time before she was going to leave this past behind her. Her mental and physical scars were losing power over her.

…A few hours later, Hashi wanted to talk to Xia about something important in the news. Xia was practically done her shift. No one else was in the bar at 4AM. Hashi approached Xia.

"So did you hear about the terrorist bombing on Terra?"

"No, what's it about?"

"Some guy blew up a whole city. He killed like, 20 people."

"Really? Home come?"

"I guess he was mad. He like, killed this Midorai girl too."

"What?"

"Yeah. Like, he had something against the Midorai people. He went crazy and killed himself along with that girl and his boyfriend."

The TV in the bar had news report of the terrorist who bombed the city.

His name… "Johov Machivellia VI."

"He looks like some pissed off Sarparian guy." Hashi said.

Xia felt a strange vibe with the picture of Johov's face displayed on the TV. Something about the way he looked made her felt nostalgic about the past.

"…Wow. He kind of… looks like… my dad."

Hashi looked back at Xia, "Your dad?"

"Yeah. My dad."

"You never told me you had a dad?"

"Yeah, I barely remember him. I was told he was a Sarparian solider and that he would later take 'ownership' over me when he came back. …but he never did."

"So you never met the guy?"

"I thought I met him. I thought I knew him. I always wanted to meet my dad. I always feel that he is somewhere out there protecting me."

Hashi's face looked upset.

"So, theres a guy that killed this Midorai girl, and you think it's your dad?"

Xia didn't know what to say.

"Whatever, thought you would like that news about your loving interest between Sarparian and Midorais. Yuck."

Hashi went to the bathroom.

Xia thought about the terrorist attack. What did this mean? Was it a bizarre event that happened out of nowhere? Did Sarparians really hated Midorais, and she was in denial about it?

…No. It's just the news. Xia continued the clean up the bar.

She thought about the earliest pictures she remembered of her dad. …He was handsome guy. A heroic man that looked liked he cared about her. He looked kind of like… Mark.

Yeah, Xia's dad must of been a pretty cool kind of guy.

…Would he have been mad that she was some alien hooker in some dirt bar? Or would he have still liked her?

Xia thought about it. "Maybe my dad loves me and thinks about me everyday. I wonder where he is?"

7.

A bright light was shining upon Johov's face. Where was he? Was he in heaven?

Johov could not move his arms. He woke from a sleep that felt like forever. He tried turning his head. Slowly, he was able to move each part of his body. What was this place?

"Are you awake?", said someone.

Johov turned his head to the side. A robot man with a large hood stood over him.

Johov could not speak. His body felt weak.

The robot walked over to the other side of the room. Johov watched him as he slowly moved from the other end.

"Where am I?", Johov said with a weak voice.

The robot man spoke back to him, "I am Zeus, welcome to the Recilliator."

Johov looked to the left and right.

Didn't he die? His body however, was perfectly fine.

"…Where am I?", Johov asked again.

Zeus sat down at the wooden desk looking at the paper files.

"…You are in the Recilliator. Did you hear that? You died once. Now you live again."

…So he did died. But he's alive again?

"…Where am I? What's going on?", Johov was too weak to say anything else.

Zeus put on his glasses checking out the documents.

"You did a good job Johov. You are a very good person. You resisted the temptations from becoming an elite MGTOW and scored a lot of girls. Good job.", Zeus said while checking out his life documents.

Johov started to move his neck and shoulders.

"It appears you did a noble deed back on Terra. …You committed a terrorist act, right?"

It was coming back to him. He blew himself up when that bitch and her boyfriend were trying to get him. Ungrateful girl. She was so beautiful too.

"You killed Prince Robjoh and his girlfriend, Chzellia. Robjoh was up to no good. He was on a mission to 'whitewash' every single women of the Midorai race. Chzellia would of been the role model for these poor girls. …You freed the Midorais from their oppression, Johov."

Johov finally stood up. He cracked his bones and moved onto his feet.

"I did what?", he asked.

"You killed Robjoh and Chzellia. You saved the Midorai race."

Johov still didn't understand what was going on.

"You are a messiah, Johov. You deserve to be resurrected."

Zeus got up from his desk and introduce himself to Johov.

"The Recilliator is a place managed by The Cult of Hades. I am Zeus, prime duke of reincarnation. You as a Sarparian that was going to live a limited life. However, you have sacrificed your morality to save the life of a greater race, the Midorai."

Johov felt like he was dreaming.

"The Midorai race will be resurrected again by you, Johov. They are dying quickly, and hardly any of them are reproducing. Your mission is to track down two people. Your child, Xia, and her mother, M'khal. Together you will form a new future society."

Johov was confused.

"Who is this Xia?", he asked.

"Your daughter, Johov. You must find Xia and rescue her from her misery. And you must find the woman of your dreams, M'khal."

"…M'khal?", Johov asked.

"The woman you raped on the battlefield. The day you lost your virginity and created a beautiful child. You have a legacy, Johov."

Zeus was talking to Johov like God was to Moses.

Johov walked across the room and looked at the window, showcasing the expansion of space.

"Where am I suppose to go?", Johov asked.

"You are going to go to the home planet of Mowo and find your legacy. You will find a place to settle down and will propagate a new race of Midorai people. It is my job to lead you in this new direction. You killed the right people, Johov. If you did not exist, Robjoh and Czehllia would of conquered the Midorai and turned them into Sarparian people. You Johov, however, will give the Midorai a new sense of power. You will create a new race of half-Sarparian-Midorai people that will start peace in the galaxy. It is up to you, Johov, to find your people."

Johov looked at Zeus. He looked back at the window.

"Come. You must come with me. I will lead you to a space pod that will launch you to Mohawaii."

Zeus hovered over to the next room. Johov followed in silence.

…They both walked down the great halls of the Recilliator. The hallway framed giant pictures of members of The Cult of Hades. Johov was amazed at the presence of such great figures. He kept following Zeus, even though he was distracted by the frames.

Johov entered a dark room with Zeus.

"Put out your arms," Zeus said.

Johov looked around. He could not see anything. Flapping his arms, Zeus put a red cape over Johov. Bright lights came on.

"You are now the new messiah that will lead the Midorai race to greatness. Please. Enter the space pod alone."

There was a space pod waiting for Johov to enter in.

Johov looked at Zeus.

"By the power of the Recilliator, you must go alone. The pod will lead you to Mowo. The rest is up to your own discovery. Go find M'khal and Xia."

Johov walked into the pod. The door closed behind him.

"The spirit of the Midorai and the Sarparian people will be reborn", Zeus said to himself.

8.

"I told you again. I'm not fucking taking out the trash! You fucking do it!", Xia yelled at Mark.

"I don't give a shit. I work all night and have to pay the bills! I didn't do anything to you!"

"I ask you to do a small goddamn favor, and you sit on your fat ass and fucking do nothing. Why don't you go fucking do it? The trash has been sitting there for three weeks!"

"Why don't you go do it? Your suppose to clean the house! I told you, I'm too fucking busy to do any of that."

"Goddamnit Mark! I can't do it myself either! Who the fuck do you think you are!?"

Xia became roommates with Mark a year ago. They started off enjoying each other's company. Mark worked the nightshifts, while Xia worked the bar. The two would be at work every single night. Unfortunately, both lost control of their intimate sides, and now, they hate each other. Xia doesn't understand Mark, and Mark doesn't understand Xia. They both had it with each other's personalities.

"I don't think I can fucking stand this anymore, Mark. I think it's time I move back with my friends!", she said to him.

"I don't get it. You want to move out now? I didn't do anything to you! All you did was yell at me!"

"You just don't get it, Mark. Your not the same person I knew! Your some trashy idiot that won't clean up after himself."

"I fucking clean up after myself! Here you go with the name calling! Do I ever call you names? No! You just bitch all the time!"

"There you go again! I can't be with someone who is not only lazy and inconsiderate of others, but as well verbally abusive. I didn't want that, Mark! I thought you were different!", Xia said while heading towards the door.

"I can't believe you think I am something I am not! I didn't do anything to you! What the hell did I do!?"

"You don't get it, do you? I loved you, Mark. Now you act like some spoiled kid that has everything. You don't care about me, you don't care about our future, and you only care about yourself. It's over Mark. Don't ever fucking call me again you meathead!", Xia slammed the door on her way out.

Mark looked dumbfounded. He was going to reach for the door and yell at her some more. Then again, what just happen?

A tear fell from Mark's eye.

…Xia stayed at Hashi's apartment. Sally moved out with Tony. Hashi was living alone.

She was so happy to see Xia at her front door. It was a surprise visit. Hashi made green tea like always. Her kitchen was the size of an old-style Japanese room, something akin to their supposed ancestors. Hashi served the tea like of a traditional "tea ceremony." Xia was sad. Hashi was like a big sister to her.

"So you broke up with him?"

"Yeah. I don't know where to go now", Xia said while taking a sip of her tea.

"You can stay here. I don't mind. I am lonely myself."

"Do you have any other boyfriends your seeing?", Xia asked.

"No. It's just a bunch of guys chasing after me like always. I get a lot of messages. I could care less. I am losing the motivation to hangout with guys. I'm getting older. Boyfriends are not for me anymore."

Xia looked down with a frown.

Hashi could understand her pain.

Xia said back, "Did you ever love someone?"

"I use to go through that phase. When I was young, I thought it was cool to be a stripper. That way, I thought the best guy would come and rescue me from my fate. But it didn't work like that, as I learned the hard way."

"They only liked you because you were…"

"No, because I was a toy for them. I always wanted to find true love. But I expected it from the wrong people. I was the only one asking for it. None of the other guys didn't care. It's a cold world out there."

Hashi's phone began to beep. She looked right at it. Xia noticed Hashi was texting someone.

"Who's that your talking too?", she said.

Hashi looked surprised.

"Oh well, it's some friend. Some guy friend."

"Another boyfriend?", Xia smiled.

"A different guy. I…" Hashi didn't know what to say.

"So you do have a boyfriend?", Xia said.

"No, I don't! It's just another guy. I don't know if he means any of it."

"Let me see a picture of him!"

Hashi was somewhat nervous. Xia grabbed Hashi's phone from her hand.

The picture was of a Sarparian man in a business suit and glasses.

Xia laughed.

"Who's he? Is he some kind of?…"

"No one. It's…", Hashi didn't know what to say.

"Is he one of those creepy clients with lots of money?", Xia said.

"No no. Not at all. Umm, we met at a Rohgo's."

"Rohgo's? You? Wait, what?", Xia was confused. (Rohgo's was a common coffee house place).

"We were talking! And… I was going there to relax and read. And like…", Hashi felt embarrassed and couldn't continue what she was saying.

Xia smiled.

"I will give you credit that he's a Sarparian guy. He does look super cute. Better than that douchebag Mark. He looks like he never committed a crime in his life."

Hashi smiled too.

"Yeah… I mean, he got his MFA in creative writing. And, he works as some real estate agent working in office… and…"

"Whoa! He's got money! Haha, are you sure your not after him for the…"

"No! Not at all! And like, he's not…"

"Did he pay you?"

"No way! I'm not joking, He's just some… nerd, who likes me", Hashi laughed.

"Really? …That's awesome," Xia chuckled.

Hashi put her phone away.

"Yeah… I really do like him. He's… He's umm…"

Hashi's secret was out. She felt like she was guilty of something.

"He's what?"

"He's a different guy, I can say that. Totally naive of everything around him, I can tell. He's really smart, and has this cute geeky thing too him thats adorable. …He told me he liked my tats. And then, like, he was telling me about Yakuza tattoos long ago and how it's about maturity… and…"

"Sounds like he has an interest in you too."

"I know right? And like, he has no tattoos! He thinks it's cute when I have tats! I mean, no Sarparian guy would ever say that… and…"

Hashi also something else to say.

"Umm… Xia. If there is one thing I learned later in life… I was totally ignoring you about. It's… Your right."

"Right about what?"

Hashi laughed, "Sarparian guys are the best! I can see why you like them."

"You like them now too!?"

"Well, I can understand why anyone would want to be with one. I mean, I avoided them back then. Until I realized, the only race of people, that are traditional, are, Sarparians! It's amazing! And this guy, he's not like, in the military or anything. He has a pretty normal and happy life I always wanted to have… and.. he's…"

"So you really do like him?", Xia said.

Hashi didn't know what to say.

"…So, why did you break up with Mark then?", she said back to Xia.

Xia was holding her tea as she sipped it.

"I can't stand him. He wasn't there when he said he was supporting me. I thought he was going to be a caring father. He wasn't. I felt like, he was using me for something else."

"And this guy is Sarparian?", Hashi asked.

"Yeah. He's Sarparian. And he's not that perfect. Your guy might be perfect, not him."

"Was he too macho, or too arrogant?"

"All of that. I think he made up stuff to get me. Don't get me wrong, we had amazing sex. But the sex is a glue that holds a relationship together. He was holding on to me, and failing to make promises as a better man. He was too arrogant in his attitude. I wish he a good person, not some meathead asshat."

Hashi noticed Xia had on a Jaasus necklace.

"Was he into Jaasus?"

Xia looked straight up at Hashi.

"No. He wasn't. He was just some guy into himself."

"I can tell if the guy is devoted if he believes in something bigger than himself. Jaasus is something Sarparian people like, and you like that stuff too, and…"

"Your right. Mark was not a Jaasus lover. That shows his true colors."

Xia held her Jaasus necklace.

"I forgot that Jaasus is forgiving. I wanted Mark to love me the same way Jaasus loves everything."

Hashi felt sympathetic towards Xia.

"You think Jaasus could save my life?", she asked Xia.

"I don't know. If you believe in him, he can."

…Xia's phone started to ring. She answered her phone.

"Hello?"

"Xia, this is Sally."

Sally called at the right time. Hashi was in the same room.

"Hey Sally. I am with Hashi at the moment."

"That's awesome! Hey, I want to tell you something."

"What's that?"

"There some guy that's been looking for you. I don't know. He's at this hostel."

"What are you doing at this hostel?"

"He called me. Please come down right now. I think it's your dad."

"My dad?"

Hash looked over at Xia. She looked back at her.

"Ok… what's happening?"

9.

Johov laid on his bed in a disgusting hostel. He wrapped himself around his red cape as a blanket.

This was it. He was finally going to meet his true love and his daughters.

Johov aborted his pod outside the city. He was able to find the nearest hostel to rest.

…That's when he started to go up to strangers and ask where a "Xia and M'khal" was.

He began his journey a week ago. Looking throughout the city of Mohawii for meaning. Johov was depressed. He was looking for a needle in an infinitely large haystack.

A nurse knocked on Johov's door.

"There is someone that would like to see you," she said like a dove.

Johov didn't feel like getting up.

"Let them come in," he said.

The nurse shut the door.

Outside in the lobby, Xia was with Sally.

"So how did this guy know about me?", she said to Sally.

"He supposedly found me online. I guess I was a 'friend' of yours, and this wackjob thinks your his daughter."

The nurse approached the two.

"You can come in his room."

"I will take care of this," Xia said to Sally.

Xia followed the nurse into Johov's room.

Xia walked into the small cell, and saw a small Sarparian man bundled in a red ball.

The nurse shut the door.

"Hello? …Hi?"

Johov twisted his head around.

"Are your Xia?"

"Yes. Yes I am."

Johov did'nt say a word, and just looked at her.

"Who are you?", she said.

"…Your my daughter," he said. "M'khal is your mother."

"…what?"

She didn't know what was going on.

"How did you know my mom?"

"I love your mom. …I raped her."

Xia didn't know what was going on. She was about to leave the room.

"Why are you stalking me?"

Johov stood up on two legs,

"I… I am your father. You look like your mother. You… I was going to come back for you. I know your mother cared for her… she was a follower of Jaasus. Do you still like Jaasus?"

Xia looked at her own cross necklace.

"…I don't get it. How do you know this?"

"…I was sent from The Cult of Hades… the… I wanted to find you. I am so happy, …I am seeing you."

Johov went in for a hug. Xia backed off.

"Who are you?", she said.

"I'm your father. My name is Johov. Please… there are real documents, that I am your father."

Xia didn't know what to do.

"Hold on," she said.

Xia left the room.

Johov again was left alone in his misery.

Outside the room, Xia was talking to the nurse.

"How is this my father?" (she was now talking in an aggressive and angry Midorai-speak with the obvious Midorai nurse)

"He knows your name, and he knows mine."

"Do you have documents on him."

"Let me check."

The nurse went over to the computer.

Xia saw that the nurse also had on Jaasus earrings.

"Do you know about his love for Jaasus?"

"Oh yeah. He said the same thing too me about my earrings."

Sally was quite concern with the issue.

"I think we should leave. This guy is some weirdo, homeless person," Sally said to Xia.

The nurse found some documents on the computer.

"Accordingly, he was a Sarparian solider. And he was in The Battle of Mowo."

"…You know, he told me, I am his daughter."

The nurse felt an overwhelming emotion.

"Really? He told me I was… I was his true love."

"…Now he likes you both," Sally said.

"Come with me," Xia said to the nurse. Both head back into the room. Sally waited outside.

The nurse and Xia entered the room. Johov looked back.

"M'khal, is that you?"

The nurse was shocked.

"…Is that your name?", Xia said.

"Yes, but, I don't know why he knows…"

"And Xia, both of you?", Johov said.

Xia looked at the nurse.

"M'khal is my mom's name. How old are you?"

The nurse looked at Xia. He could tell Xia was an attractive girl in her early 20s. M'khal, a mentally disturbed and worn-out nurse, was still working her job… and yet sh had beautiful, motherly charm about her.

"…They took my daughter away from me when I was young…"

"I love you M'khal!", Johov went up to hug the nurse.

M'khal took the hug.

Xia saw something within the two.

"I know who both of you are. M'khal, they took your daughter and sold her into slavery. They told you to work as a nurse and denied your right to be a mother. I was left alone on Terra… and I was depressed for years. All I wanted was true love. I'm so sorry this has happened. I love you both and want to take care of you as a father!"

Johov looked like he was about to tear up.

The nurse looked back at Xia.

She said, *"Bawa-shi mi-taku mi-do-desu."*

In a peculiar Midorai-speak, Xia remembered what she was saying.

272

"...*Bawa da'hal fur-shika?*," Xia said back.

Xia remember those words when she was a kid.
The little *taku* she was. The *hans-flower.* Her mother would call her that.

...Was this nurse her mother?

ἐπίλογος.

Johov's mission was finally completed. He rejoined together with his wife and daughter. Together they were a family.

Saparian man, a Midorai wife, and a mixed daughter.

M'khal was shocked to learn that Johov was her rapist. She erased the memory a long time ago. She was disenchanted and disturb by her rape. She tried to justified her rape with the creation of her daughter. The man who called himself Johov proclaimed M'khal as his true love. M'khal always wanted a man to enter her life. But the rapist now told her that "I love you." M'khal had to surrender towards his supernatural will. Johov was a kind and forgiving man that wanted to be love. M'khal always wanted to be loved. The same way Jaasus had once preached.

…M'khal, who often dreamed about being raped by handsome man, was joined together with her true love.

Xia was happy to see her mother again. M'khal looked so much like Xia. Over the years, M'khal's cheeks grew, like

274

two rosey apples. Her body was thick. Xia could tell that her mom was chased after by the Midorai men in her younger years. Her thighs grew that would perfectly fit the stereotypical hot mom nurse. Her earrings, and the way M'khal's hair was groomed, made her look like she was in her early 20's. Her tits were fat and comfortable to lay on. Xia had small, yet large titties attached onto her small body. M'khal and her daughter would of made the perfect fuck duo together.

It was a Sarparian man who took M'khal's virginity away. Johov was lucky to have beautiful wife and a daughter.

His next objective was obvious.

Johov bought an estate from the aristocratic elite. This money was donated by The Cult of Hades.

On this land, Johov built a house.

Xia and M'khal began bounding with one another. Soon, Sally and Hashi moved in with their Sarparian boyfriends. One step at a time.

Johov would slowly woo over the trust of Xia. Xia would learn the trade of nursing from her mom. Two years later, she would become a nurse under M'khal's training.

Xia met a handsome Severian doctor, who she wedded a year later.

Johov's estate grew. Four couples of Sarparian-Midorais lived here.

Every year, on April the 20th, Johov announce a day where the estate couples would have sex. In return, a few months later, they would all have new children. A new race of Midorai people, mixed with the blood of the Sarparians.

M'khal, who was a little too old to have kids, was able to conceive a new child, and a little sister for Xia, named M'wado.

Xia conceived a daughter, Alexandria.

Sally conceived a son, Roshi.

Hashi conceived twins, Jack and W'ani.

Every year, by Johov's command, the couples would have sex, and have more children.

M'khal could only conceive two more girls, Z'alo and Ami.

Within 12 years, each couple had 10 children.

Xia's offspring included: Alexandria, Rome, Hana, Natsume, Kat, Joe, Sylvie, Sally, Hashi, and Erika.

Sally's offspring included: Roshi, Masu, John, Inoue, Oscar, Xia, Alice, Skylar, Jenny, and Chris.

Hashi's offspring included: Z'alo, Ami, Lily, Orrendi, Aka, Kawai, Chi'wa, Sarah, Stacy, and David.

M'khal, Xia, Sally and Hashi acted as teachers for their children. The husbands went upon their daily jobs and told other friends about the newly founded religion and culture they were apart of.

When the offspring reach the age of 20, and the girls of 18, each child was assigned a lover from the other family. Both the males and females would be paired to have sex on the day of April the 20th.

Within it's first year, the offspring was multiplied. It was the duty of these children to take care and raise their own family one day. Everything was assigned and arranged.

The Midorai community soon acknowledged Johov's estate to be a village of it's own.

It was Johov who stopped the Sarparian domination of the Midorai mind. He was able to assimilate the Midorai into a new race. The Midorai were now more powerful with Sarparians blood. A new race of people.

…Laying on his death bed, Johov issued a bible, an esoteric textbook about the history of the Johovians. A history of the greatness of both the Sarparian and Midorai races meeting together for the first time. This book would be called The Giga Johvox. Compiled together the memories and stories of the Midorai and Sarparians who joined in union. Johov, on his death bed, said that he loved M'khal. He gave M'khal a kiss one final time. M'khal would take his place as a ruling matriarchy. Then following Xia to take her place.

"The flowers that bloomed all around us, growing after the rape of M'khal. God bless this fragile life."

Pilleater is an young avant-garde artist. He graduated from Temple University in 2016 and lives outside of Philadelphia. Pilleater currently blogs both on his social media and website.

https://choamcharity.bandcamp.com

www.youtube.com/pilleater

www.twitter.com/realpilleater

www.instagram.com/pilleater

Other fun facts:

-Subscribed to Juxtapoz Magazine and Giant Robot at age 13, which changed his life.

-Bought a Merzbow record and was Flash cartooning at 14.

-Met Tim Biskup and Aaron Kraten at 15.

-Was a popular, hipster chiptune musician at 16. (*Myspace fame and live shows*)

-Got into digital hardcore and white nationalism at 17. (*A young pilleater can be spotted in a classic Realicide live video*)

-First blowjob at 18.

-Drummer in a grindcore band at 19.

-Professional Android: Netrunner player at 20.

-Full-time Asian studies Junior at 21.

-Co-host for The Stark Truth with Robert Stark at 22. (www.starktruthradio.com)

...and now, there is this book!

www.ingramcontent.com/pod-product-compliance
Lightning Source LLC
Chambersburg PA
CBHW031114030726
47496CB00002BA/534